THE QUICKENING MAZE

THE QUICKENING MAZE

Adam Foulds

WINDSOR
PARAGON

First published 2009
by Jonathan Cape
This Large Print edition published 2010
by BBC Audiobooks Ltd
by arrangement with
The Random House Group Ltd

Hardcover   ISBN: 978 1 408 46122 8
Softcover   ISBN: 978 1 408 46123 5

British Library Cataloguing in Publication Data available

Printed and bound in Great Britain by
CPI Antony Rowe, Chippenham and Eastbourne

to my parents

Prologue: The World's End

He'd been sent out to pick firewood from the forest, sticks and timbers wrenched loose in the storm. Light met him as he stepped outside, the living day met him with its details, the scuffling blackbird that had its nest in their apple tree.

Walking towards the wood, the heath, beckoning away. Undulations of yellow gorse rasped softly in the breeze. It stretched off into unknown solitudes.

He was a village boy and he knew certain things. He thought that the edge of the world was a day's walk away, there where the cloud-breeding sky touched the earth at the horizon. He thought that when he got there he would find a deep pit and he would be able to look down into it and see the world's secrets. Same as he knew he could see heaven in water, a boy on his knees staring into the heavy, flexing surface of the gravel-pit ponds or at a shallow stream flashing over stones.

He set off, down into the wide yellow fragrance. The wood he could collect on his return.

Soon he was further from the village than he had ever been, furthest from the tough, familiar nest of his cottage. He walked quite out of his knowledge, into a world where the birds and flowers did not know him, where his shadow had never been.

It confused him. He started to think that the sun was shining in a new quarter of the sky. He felt no fear yet: the sun lit wonders in a new zone that held him in steady rapt amazement. He did wonder, though, why the old world had not come to an end, why the horizon was no closer.

He walked and walked and before he'd thought the morning passed, the light was thickening.

ix

Moths flittered under the bushes. Frogs fidgeted along the rabbit tracks and mice twittered their little splintery cries. Overhead trembled the first damp stars.

It was the hour of waking spirits. Now he was afraid.

He hurried around with a panicking heart and found behind him a splay of paths. By chance he got on the right one. As the darkness grew, gathering first in the bushes and trees, then soaking out from them, he found himself approaching his own village. At least it looked like his own village, but somehow the distance he'd travelled made him uncertain. It looked the same. It definitely was the same, but somehow it didn't seem right, in place. Even the church, rising over the wood, the church he'd seen every day as soon as he could see at all, looked counterfeit. Frightened, racing, like a lost bird he flung his light body towards what he hoped was home.

His name. He heard his name being called. John! John! Jo-ohn! Village voices. He could put names to them all. He ran now, not answering, to his own cottage, feeling a tumult of relief as he approached. When he stepped through the open doorway his mother yelped at the sight and flew towards him. Her strong arms encircled him, her bosom crushed against his face.

'We thought you was dead. In the wood. They're out looking for you. We thought you was struck down by a falling . . . Oh, but you're home.'

Autumn

Abigail started neatly at a walk as her mother had just smartened her, plucking and smoothing her dress into place. She had run a fingertip down Abigail's nose as she bent down with a crackle of her own dress and repeated the message to carry. But outside the door and with the sun warm through the trees and the path firm under her tightly laced boots, Abigail couldn't help it: after a few paces she broke into a run.

She ran across the garden and over into the grounds of Fairmead House, then along its side and past the pond where Simon the idiot was throwing stones; even she knew he'd been told not to do that. He looked round sharply at the sound of her footsteps just after he'd launched one. It couldn't be stopped: their eyes met at the moment it plopped in and slow circles widened across the green water. It was only the child, though. He smiled naughtily at her, knowing she wouldn't tell. She ran round the corner past Mr Stockdale the attendant whom she did not like. He was large and strict and when he tried to play with her it was not meant, not meant properly, and his hands were heavy. But there was Margaret sitting on a stool, sewing. She liked Margaret, her thin, sharp-chinned face like a wooden toy, and wide, clear, kind eyes. She was a peaceful lady, mostly, and now Abigail walked over and leaned against her knees to be for a moment inside that calm. Margaret didn't say anything, stroked once the back of Abigail's head as the child looked down at her sampler. There were three colours of thread: green for hills, brown for the cross and black for

3

lines coming out of the cross. Abigail put out a finger and felt the bumpy black stitches. 'God's love,' Margaret whispered. 'Beams.' Briefly she wound the thread she was working with a couple of times around Abigail's finger. 'Wrap you up in it.'

Abigail smiled. 'Good day,' she said and set off running again, past some others strolling there, and then when she saw him, with greater speed towards her father.

Matthew Allen swung the axe down onto the upturned log. The blade sunk down into it, but it didn't split, so he raised the axe and log together and brought them down hard. The log flew apart into two even pieces that rocked on the grass. 'Nothing to it,' he remarked. He stooped and added the new pieces with their clean white pith to the barrow and stood another log on the stump.

Seeing Abigail bouncing towards him, he handed the lunatic the axe and grappled her up into his arms. 'Just go on like that until you've filled the barrow, please.'

Abigail could feel the warmth of his body through its compress of clothes. She wriggled at the sensation of his humid whiskers against her as he kissed her cheek.

'Mother says to come now because they'll be here pleasantly.'

Allen smiled. 'Did she say "pleasantly" or "presently"?'

Abigail frowned. 'Presently,' she said.

'Then we'd better set off.'

Abigail leaned her head into his neck, into the smell of him in his cravat, and felt her feet swinging in the air with each of his steps, like riding a pony.

4

Patients greeted her father with a nod as he passed or with some rearrangement of their posture. Simon the idiot, who definitely was not throwing stones into the pond, waved with his whole arm.

Outside the house Hannah stood waiting, holding her sharp elbows and thoughtfully drawing a line on the path in front of her with the toe of her boot. She looked up at them as they arrived and spoke as if to justify herself.

'I thought I ought to wait to greet them, given that there was no one else.'

Allen laughed. 'I'm sure even a poet is capable of pulling a door bell.' He watched his daughter ignore the comment, staring at the ground. Abigail was twisting in his arms now the ride was over, and he set her down. She ran off a few yards to pick up an interesting stick. The front door opened and Mrs Allen walked out to join them. 'Fine weather,' she commented.

'Are we not too many now?' Hannah asked. 'The brother may be a little overwhelmed.'

'They both might be,' her father rejoined. 'But a warm family welcome will do neither of them any harm.'

'I'll only wait with you a moment,' Eliza Allen said. 'I've things to do, only I saw you all standing out here in the sun. Oh, look, there's Dora seeing us now.'

Hannah turned and saw her sister's face in the window. She wouldn't come out, Hannah knew. She didn't like extraordinary people. She liked ordinary people and was preparing for her wedding, after which she could live almost entirely among them. She retreated out of sight like a fish from the surface of a pond, leaving the glass dark.

'Abi, put that down,' her mother instructed. 'And don't wipe your hands on your pinafore. Come here.' Abigail joined them in a mildly shamed, dilatory way and allowed her mother to clean her palms with a handkerchief. 'Where's Fulton?' Eliza asked her husband.

'He's occupied, I'm sure. We don't have to be all arranged here like this. We're not having our portrait painted.'

This was not how Hannah had arranged this meeting in her imagination. She would not have had the clutter of her family around her, not at first, and she would have happened by at the right moment, or at least could have easily dissembled her preceding vigilance. She could have been a solitary, attractive girl of seventeen, a wood nymph even, discovered in her wandering. She stared along the road as far as she could: it turned sharply to the right a little way ahead and the forest cut off the view down the hill. Through the trees she felt them approaching, an event approaching. Who knew how significant it might prove to be? She should try to expect less; there was little chance it would match her hopes. But it might. Certainly, something was about to happen. People were about to arrive.

And then it was happening. The carriage from Woodford was approaching, trunks strapped to its roof, the horses bowing their way up the hill, the driver dabbing at their broad backs with his whip. Quickly, hoping not to be seen, Hannah pinched colour into her cheeks. Mrs Allen picked up Abigail and held her on her hip. Matthew Allen smoothed his whiskers with both hands, tugged his waistcoat down, and enriched the swell of his cravat.

As the carriage slowed beside them, the driver touching the brim of his hat, Matthew Allen stepped forward and opened the door. 'Misters Tennyson,' he said in his deeper, professional voice. 'Welcome to High Beach.'

A cough and a thank you was heard from the shadowy interior where long limbs were moving.

Hannah stood a little closer to her mother as the two brothers emerged.

The two Tennysons were tall, clean-shaven and darkly similar. They greeted the three females with courteous bows. Hannah felt close to saying something, but didn't. She heard her mother say, 'Gentlemen, welcome.' One Tennyson mumbled a reply as they both stood blinking, shifting on their feet after the confinement of the carriage. Both began lighting pipes.

The trunks were unfastened and brought down by Dr Allen and one of the Tennysons. Both the Tennysons were handsome, one perhaps more sensitive in appearance than the other—would that be the poet or the melancholic? Hannah waited for them to speak some more. She wanted desperately to know which of these two men her interest should fall upon.

*   *   *

John woke up without any feeling down one side. He reached a hand up to his face to feel for the rough crusting of frost and drag it off, but there was none. So either he wasn't outside or the weather was mild. He felt that the air wasn't

7

moving over him, wasn't alive. He was inside, in a shut room.

He kept his eyes closed, floating there in his own inner darkness, wanting to delay the knowledge of which room he was in, although in truth he knew. But it might not be there, it might be the right room, with Patty first up from the bed and busy with the children.

He opened his eyes by fractions and saw a dark grey room. The imagined biting rime on his sky side was the old numbness from sleeping out years ago, not a real touch of the world, and he wasn't home. There was the window, glowing dimly with wet autumn light. It showed its view of two trees bent by the wavery glass.

Below he could hear other inmates moving and the brisk voice of Mrs Allen. She would collect him shortly to accompany her across the garden to the doctor's house for breakfast, him having been a good lad.

He lifted the blanket, swung his softening white feet onto the clean wood floor, and stood up, and immediately wanted to lie back down again and not lie back down again and go and not go anywhere and not be there and be home.

*   *   *

John spread butter thickly on his bread and bit. Those considered constitutionally able had cutlets to eat and sawed at their meat, including Charles Seymour, the aristocrat who wasn't mad at all. He'd condescended to join them this morning. The doctor had listed his pedigree to the new man as though presenting a prize mastiff. There had been

8

polite talk, mostly about Cambridge, that lucky, unknown world, while John said nothing. Now the table was silent. George Laidlaw was talking to himself, almost inaudibly, his lips fluttering with his habitual fantastical calculations of the National Debt. Fulton Allen ate with a lad's appetite, sweeping up juices with a chunk of bread on his fork. Margaret ate morsels silently. Hannah Allen kept glancing at the new man, Septimus Tennyson, whose head trembled and whose gaze seemed too sensitive to look at anything for long, but shrivelled back from what it hit like a snail's wizening eyes. Tall and faded he looked. Why didn't Hannah glance instead at John? He licked silky butter from his teeth and would much rather have been eating her, the prettyish, pale thing. He wondered how she tasted in the nest between her legs. He'd have liked to see her cheeks flush and hear her startled breath. The doctor smiled over his chewing at everyone. 'Do we all have plenty to do today? George, you'll be working in the vegetable garden, won't you?'

*　　　*　　　*

John lay in the warmth of the bath, nursing the whiteness of his belly. He pressed his fingers into it, forming ridges of soft dough. Beneath, his penis had bobbed up out of the water and was capped with ticklish cold air. He lay back, the water slopping up beside his ears, and let his arms float. He lay so still he could feel his heartbeats shunting a little force around his body.

Knuckles beat against the door. 'Five minutes, Mr Clare.'

Peter Wilkins was an old attendant. His heavy face was pouched and drooping. The lower lids of his watery eyes hung so low that they showed a quarter of an inch of their red lining like a worn-out coat with failing seams. He had had his fill of restrainings, bathings, arguings, and had now taken upon himself the duty of keeping the gate. He never mentioned that this was now what he understood his job to be in case he was contradicted and had his former duties imposed. Instead, each morning he walked purposefully, but not too quickly or obviously, to the gate under its trees and stood there.

His face was so detailed, so full of character, that John always found encountering him to be a small event, like eating something. John thanked Wilkins with a raised hat as he let him go out towards his work.

He walked with the quick skimming steps of a labourer up the hill to the admiral's garden, getting a little heat and motion into his flesh. He began whistling a tune, 'Tie a Yellow Handkercher', one of those he'd transcribed years ago from gypsies and old boys, for a volume that no one would publish, that died on a desk in a cramped London office. Thus the real life of the people goes insulted and ignored. He sang out loud 'Flash company been the ruin o' me and the ruin o' me quite', then stopped: he was feeling it too strongly and it was more imprisonment to simplify himself like that in other people's words, not when he had so many of his own. Also, he'd seen two charcoal burners on the road ahead, round-shouldered and dirty, their faces blackened and featureless. He angled his hat down and skulked under it as they passed, then wondered if that would have made them more or less likely to take him for one of the mad.

When they'd gone, he looked up again into the forest. Wet. Not much stirring. A flicker of wings. Mist between the crooked trees.

*   *   *

As he worked the admiral's garden a robin joined him. It darted forward to needle the earth he'd turned, watching him, waiting, poised on its little thready legs. John saw the throb of a worm by his spade, plucked it up, and threw it at the bird. The robin flew away, flew back, and jabbed at the meal.

Watching this, being there, given time, the world revealed itself again in silence, coming to him. Gently it breathed around him its atmosphere: vulnerable, benign, full of secrets, his. A lost thing returning. How it waited for him in eternity and almost knew him. He'd known and sung it all his life. Perception of it now, amid all his truancy and suffering, made his eyes thicken with warm tears.

Too easily moved—he knew that. Nervous and excitable. He dried himself on his sleeve and went back to working, the easy rhythm and weight through his arms. A painless prescription. And it was light work, nothing compared to lime burning or threshing. He hacked down on a clod of this thick Essex clay and remembered the light flail his father had made him when he was a boy. Standing beside the old man's effortless fast rhythm of circling whacks he'd tried to keep up, his arm burning, his shirt sweated through, his damp skin furred with itchy grain dust. Weak but willing, his father called him.

'Good afternoon, John, or morning.'

It was the admiral, standing very dignified and straight. John had always suspected that he stood straighter and with greater dignity now in his retirement than he had on the seas. He looked spick and span, very comprehensively brushed, the remnants of his grey hair all shooting forwards from his crown, his long blue coat as spotless as a horse before a show. A man who'd known Nelson. 'And how are we today?'

John stood up, his earthen five feet two feeling very shabby and insufficient opposite the admiral. 'Very good, sir. Fine day.'

'Indeed.' The admiral released one hand from behind his back and gestured out at the woods. Like a dog, John looked at the hand, not at the direction indicated. He'd forgotten how twisted and swollen the admiral's hands were, fingers like lengths of ginger root. John wondered that he didn't wear gloves, but perhaps he couldn't get them on. 'Yes,' the admiral said, 'it's the fine sort of autumn weather. I have an invitation in town,' he announced. John bowed at the fact. 'So I'm off to Woodford to entrust my poor person to the train.' The admiral smiled.

John also smiled. 'I wish you a safe journey,' he said.

'Yes,' the admiral said slowly. He seemed not to like the concerned sincerity of this response. The thought of his bodily destruction at unnatural speed was not meant actually to be entertained.

12

'Yes, indeed. So I shall bid you good day. Please convey my regards to the doctor and Mrs Allen. Oh, yes, there's someone taking Beech Hill House, a friend of the doctor's, I believe. Do you by any chance know who?'

'I'm afraid not, sir.'

'Ah well. Anon, then.'

The admiral let the gate clap behind him and headed down the hill, his thick hands bunched in the small of his back.

John whistled enviously after him 'Flash company been the ruin o' me and the ruin o' me quite'. An evening in London with the old, wild lads—that was what he needed. He felt his flesh strain towards the thought of beer, wanting drunkenness, wanting the world softened and flowing around him. To be back in his green jacket, the country clown for his friends from *The London Magazine* with their bristling literary talk, their sharp, rehearsed epigrams scattered like cut stones through the thickness of talk. And later, swaggering, scenes around them changing like backcloths flown up and down in a tatty theatre until he found himself with a plump young something, her nest tickling his nose as he strained the root of his tongue, tasting up into her, then quenching himself inside her, that wonderful release, hugging her as he did so, rubbing the sweat-loosened paint from her cheek onto his own.

He could look up an address or two and find the old gang, balder, plumper, more fitfully employed now that the magazine had folded. But no point: it was gone, and he couldn't have gone anyway, he reminded himself. He was an inmate, a prisoner. He was due back at Allen's. At present, it was

13

enough to have got through the day. But the thought of it all made him want to kick. And Nature had taken herself away from his dirty little fury and left him there.

He worked until dusk and walked back. Peter Wilkins opened the gate for him. 'You'd better hurry,' he told him, 'or you'll be late for evening prayers.'

* * *

Charles Seymour sat at his desk and wrote. His valet, with almost nowhere to resort to in this wretched place, lingered behind him, standing like a sentry against the wall.

> . . . You counsel me to console myself with the thought of my freedom. I see how you struggle, my little darling, to smile encouragingly at me through your tears, but do not think I believe your heart is in it. Nevertheless, let me answer to that. First of all, to be stuck in an establishment such as this . . .

He dipped his pen, stared at the wall.

> . . . seems a very peculiar definition of freedom. I am imprisoned in a madhouse and in my right mind and imprisoned in my desire.

He stopped and looked down at this extravagance, but did not scratch it out.

> I was brought to this hellhole by my father to

14

prevent us marrying and still I remain here. I know that you are referring to my freedom from obligation, viz. my freedom from you. I needn't tell you that to me that is no liberty at all. What is my freedom for, if I cannot have what I desire? It is a useless burden, if it can be said to exist at all . . .

*　　　*　　　*

Was He beyond the trees?

Of course He must be in them, through them, as they were His creation, but Margaret did not feel that. Having known Him in the actual live Spirit, she was no stickler for orthodoxy and knew what she knew. She felt Him infinitely behind the trees, behind matter, and the trees stood up as a guard, a brake. Their limbs reached into each other, preventing her, manufacturing darkness in the heart of the wood. No, not darkness—she must be proportionate, clear-minded to receive Him—but twilight. Their trivial falling leaves coloured the air.

She was a poor creature with sin's stink on her and must sit and wait on the far side of unbearable distance. That distance was larger than any in the mere world alone. It was absolute. But there was comfort there: the distance was a sign of His mastery and power. The wall that separated them connected them also, joined them by separation. In her inmost nearness that distance touched her and hurt her and was itself a revelation of Him. It was something she could hang on to.

Margaret stretched a fresh piece of muslin across the frame and fixed it there. Several samplers were

15

already piled on the small table of her room. Soon she would give them away. They were weak signals of the Truth, but she was soothed by making them, by the image of the cross forming starkly in front of her and the purring of the thread drawn through the cloth. It was a task that sealed her spirit in contemplation until she couldn't hear the shouts of the mad or the weather, the branches grinding and clicking in the wind.

But how long would she have to wait? She might die. She might die and never know it again and be forgotten in darkness.

Margaret wondered if she should start to fast once more.

*   *   *

Alfred Tennyson screwed in his monocle, stooped and peered closely at the phrenological bust on top of Matthew Allen's writing desk. He read a few of the labels on the glossy surface of the head that named the mental organs corresponding with that area. Amativeness. Agreeableness. Ideality. The whole bland, stereotyped human head was speckled with these faculties.

'Ah, that, well,' Matthew Allen, who was talking rapidly, changed the course of his speech as he saw his guest examining this medical ornament. 'I'm increasingly of the opinion that these categories are by and large symbolical. There may be an overall rightness of attribution, but I can't say that in my clinical work I've found watertight correspondences. The map is useful, however, for keeping in mind the panoply of things to be considered.'

16

'I had my bumps read once,' Tennyson said. 'And was not dazzled by any brilliance of analysis. The fellow rather overestimated my quantity of animal spirits, perhaps because I'm large and was with friends after a lunch where let's say some wine was consumed.'

'Indeed. Indeed, there are vulgar practitioners out there, in their hundreds now, but really they aren't to be thought of. Vauxhall Gardens stuff.'

Matthew Allen looked round, wondering what to draw his guest's attention to next. He felt excitable at the literary young man's presence in his private study and was eager to impress upon him the range of his researches. He watched Tennyson relight his pipe, hollowing his clean-shaven cheeks as he plucked the flame upside down into the bowl of scorched tobacco. The head was massive and handsome undeniably, with a dark burnish to the skin. Behind the dome of the forehead, strongly suggestive of intellectual power, very promising poems were being formed. He was very different in appearance to poor little Clare, but the forehead was reminiscent. The poet had been right about himself—he did seem deficient in animal spirits. The case was not nearly so morbid as his brother Septimus's, but Alfred Tennyson also moved slowly, as though through a viscous medium of thought, of doubt. Being so short-sighted might have exacerbated that, the world dim and untrustworthy around him.

As Matthew Allen stood diagnosing his guest, Tennyson now reached out and picked up a mineral sample. He brought it close to his monocle, saw its many metallic facets. It was a glittering tumble of right angles, little walls and

17

roofs jutting out from each other like a town destroyed by an earthquake.

'Iron pyrites,' Allen explained. 'I've many other samples you'll see ranged around the room. My intention was, is still, to collect samples of every mineral to be found in the British Isles, but I have quite a few more to go. Chemistry was for a while a subject of mine. Here,' Allen paced quickly across the rug to a shelf, ran a finger across spines until he found five slender identical volumes. He pulled one out. 'My lectures on chemistry. I gave them in Scotland some years ago. Carlyle—do you know Carlyle?—Thomas Carlyle, he attended, as I recall. I knew him even back then in our Edinburgh days. Perhaps I could take you to Chelsea and introduce you.'

'I've had the pleasure of making his acquaintance, and Jane's, already.'

'Oh, very good. Well then, perhaps we should visit together. It really is very straightforward now with the train at Woodford.'

Tennyson opened the volume that Allen handed to him. He read a line or two about the flow of the caloric from heated objects. He knew something of the theories from his own reading in the library at Somersby, shut away from the clamour of family and pets, with nothing to do but continue his education with as much self-discipline as he could muster. But he wouldn't have dared pronounce on the subject. Evidently the doctor was a man of scope and capacity. And they had friends in common.

'Caloric flow,' he murmured as he surfaced from the book.

'Indeed, indeed,' the doctor enthused. 'My

18

contention in this work, as elsewhere, is that there is behind the phenomenon of the caloric, behind all phenomena, a principal cause I nominate The Grand Agent.'

'The Grand Agent.'

'Yes. A common cause, a unitary force. There is a union through all things. Heat and light are manifestations, as are living organisms and their animal spirits.'

'Energy. Thoughts.'

'Yes, thoughts as well. Their energy—the flow of them.'

'I see. A Spinozism, of sorts.' And Tennyson did see: a white fabric, candescent, pure, flowing through itself, surging, charged, unlimited. And in the world the flourishing of forms, their convulsions: upward thrive of trees, sea waves, the mathematical toys of sea shells, the flight of dragonflies. It all changed constantly. 'All the metamorphoses of living beings,' Tennyson said, gesturing at the window with his pipe.

'Precisely,' Allen said, beaming. 'The forest is a perfect example.'

The forest died into itself, growing, shapes fading, eaten, lengthening anew. Yes, yes. And thought, the unbreaking wave, constantly changing—colours, shapes, sinuously pouring towards the world, pulsing with language.

'And unliving things, inorganic things have their energy also.'

'My philosophical speculations tend to the same view,' Tennyson went on.

'Oh, that's interesting. As a poet, you feel . . .'

'As a boy,' Tennyson began, catching the enthusiasm, feeling released now beyond the polite

19

chatter of acquaintances into the deep, the frictionless element of real thought. 'As a boy I could put myself into a trance by repeating my name over and over until my sense of identity was quite dissolved. What I was then was a being somehow merging, or sustained, with a greater thing, truly vast. It was abstract, warm, featureless and frightful.'

'The Grand Agent?'

'Perhaps, perhaps. Well, certainly actually. I mean to say, if we're right about this at all, then what else would it be?'

Dr Allen did not say 'a mental phenomenon'. For a moment they simply smiled at each other. How remarkable and exhilarating to have found their deepest speculations reflected in the other, about the universe, about existence.

'It would be nice,' Allen said, 'if we were able to talk some more. Are you now intending to stay?'

'Oh, yes. I agreed to take the house yesterday.'

'Oh, marvellous. Splendid. Well, no doubt you'll be a great addition to Epping society, such as it is. And of course you'll be near Septimus and that will be a great benefit to him.'

Tennyson inclined his head at the mention of his suffering brother. The blush of enthusiasm left him, dwindling down painfully to a small heat of embarrassment. That often came after too intense a disclosure of self with somebody; now it was made the more intense by the thought of Septimus. The wide line of his mouth hardened. Allen saw and sought to reassure him.

'I've no doubt that Septimus has very fine prospects of recovery. Melancholy, you know, the English malady, what you will, is really quite

20

tractable, I've found. Brightness of company, exercise, a familial atmosphere, an unbosoming of anxieties . . .'

'Unbosoming?'

'Yes, the disclosure of personal fears and unhappinesses. Often I find encouraging patients through a conversational, what shall we call it, memoir is terribly useful.'

Tennyson huffed out a big mouthful of uninhaled smoke. 'So you'll be hearing all about my family.'

'Probably. But I make no certain inferences from the testimony of unhappy individuals. That really isn't the point. At any rate, families, well . . .' He smiled. 'Nowhere more productive of mental difficulty. I attach no shame to coming from one. It is not a matter in which we generally have a choice.'

'You'll see. You'll be mired in it. The black blood of the Tennysons.'

'So there is a predisposition—to melancholy, or other disturbances? Very often . . .'

'There are quieter barnyards. Somehow we don't take life easily.'

'Ah.' Matthew Allen tilted his head and stood still, waiting to allow Tennyson to go on with what he was saying.

'I accompanied my brother, you see, because I thought I might be entering your establishment myself. And now I've decided to stay in this area, this different atmosphere.'

'Oh, yes?'

'Yes. Away. Although these woods are rather gloomy.'

'Oh, time of year. They blossom, you know, they put out green leaves.'

21

Tennyson, who had already filled the room with thickly drifting smoke, again relit his pipe.

'There is no shame in encountering these difficulties. In some sense, quite the reverse. They argue a great mental power that is prone to exhaust itself, in creation, in your case, I would imagine. You know of other cases, I imagine, among poets.'

'Of course. So. The price to be paid.'

'But it needn't be exorbitant.' Allen smiled. 'I'm very pleased you've come to visit me here and have had a glimpse of my interests. I ought to spend more time on them. I suspect I've made the breakthroughs I will make in therapy for the insane. After that is the long work of practice, which tires after a while.'

'Indeed?'

'Oh, I'm committed to it, of course. But I feel the need for a new something, to research and create again. And of course, money is never not a concern, with a family, property.'

'Oh, yes? I've no doubt you have the brain to find something.'

'And to return to what we were saying earlier, I think it is unhelpful to specialise too strictly. One must have a broad range of intellectual activities if one is seeking unifying ideas. Bacon's the man.'

'Indeed? I have a Cambridge friend who is editing him. Perhaps I could arrange for you to meet.'

'Well, that would be wonderful. Thank you,' Allen said and rather fervently shook the young poet's hand. 'Actually, perhaps you will walk with me. I have a patient I must see.'

Seated by the window with their books piled ready, to pass the time Annabella sketched a bust of Hannah. They were waiting for Mademoiselle Leclair, their French tutor, who hardly seemed a mademoiselle. She was a dumpy spinster from somewhere in Picardy with a pale extensive face that ran mostly downhill from a long, white nose. The girls were too old for this tuition, but continued on improving themselves as they prepared for marriage. Mademoiselle Leclair knew that the classes were a genteel diversion and her manner was kind and encouraging, always patient with the girls' *bêtises*. Hannah often felt ashamed when she noticed her thick shoulders or the sour warmth of her breath as she read.

Not that Hannah Allen was entirely pleased with her own appearance. On the whole, she passed: she was slender, fair-haired; her bosom was decent. Smaller than her sister Dora's, it was also lighter, less motherly. Her pallor, however, was just the far side of attractive. Of course, it was from her Scottish ancestry and that gave it welcome, even enviable associations of Byron and Scott, but the whiteness of her face made her lips look a little bloody. Also her teeth, which were really a perfectly normal colour, looked yellowish in contrast. Her eyelashes were blond. Her eyebrows looked like summer wheat.

Hannah felt a tingling at Annabella's scrutiny, the flicker of her gaze over her as she drew. She watched Annabella's dark eyes lift from the page and meet her own, then realised their gazes hadn't quite met: Annabella stared impersonally at some portion of Hannah's face. Annabella was herself unequivocally beautiful, really exquisite, and to a degree that made Hannah puzzle over precisely what it comprised, what made someone beautiful. Beauty was so fugitive and variable in so many people and among her father's patients she'd seen many an example of it extinguished, distorted or reversed, but there in Annabella it sat and stayed all day. She was always beautiful. Her complexion was lovely, with just the right susceptibility to blushes. Her eyes were large and dark. her lips were full, particularly the lower one, and they were always like that without any arrangement or pouting on Annabella's part. If Hannah had been a man, she was sure that she would have wanted to kiss her. It was her neck that decisively elevated her up out of the realm of normal good looks. It was long, slender, and curved gracefully up from her shoulders. Fine curls of her dark hair, escaping from its pins, rested on her nape. The sight of them made Hannah feel tender towards Annabella, as though she were a child, but also sensual. If she'd been anything other than negligent of her appearance, almost oblivious to it, she would have been unbearable. As it was, her great power of beauty was only ever noticeable in her effect on other people, never in her. She was Hannah's true and best friend, and had been since they were little girls, since the Allens had moved to Epping. Annabella lived in a calm, small house in the forest not far from Hannah's own. Her father was a magistrate, a respectable man to whom Matthew Allen had paid his respects on arriving. Discovering the pretty, demure child of Hannah's age, he'd encouraged them together and since then

24

they'd gone on growing upwards, twining together. Hannah had already confided in Annabella the news of Mr Alfred Tennyson's arrival.

'Have you seen him again?' she asked.

'He's been to the house, to see my father, but I missed him.'

'Shame.' Annabella smiled. 'Tell me what he's like again.'

Hannah laughed. 'Like a poet, I think.'

'What, little and plump like that Mr Clare?'

'No,' Hannah responded vehemently. 'No. Anyway, Mr Clare was a peasant poet, and Alfred Tennyson,' Hannah loved unfurling the long banner of his name, 'isn't that. I mean to say that he's pensive, brooding you might say. Tall.'

'How tall is he?'

'Tall. Six feet or more.'

'And handsome?'

'Annabella.'

'Well, is he?'

'Yes, he is. Dark. Strong shoulders. Clean-shaven. He wears a cape and a wide-brimmed hat. He looks rather like a Spaniard.'

'You've never seen a Spaniard.'

'I've read. Everyone is familiar with the colouring of the typical Spaniard.'

'Everybody's familiar with the colouring of the typical Spaniard,' Annabella repeated. The girls were at an age of hectic imitation, mimicking people's phrases and gestures to each other, mostly satirically, sometimes attempting to carry them off. When no one else was around, they mirrored each other.

'Now is he married or engaged?'

Hannah shrieked. 'Annabella!'

'Do not, please, feign a scandalised tone. We are seventeen. We have to be thinking of these things. What we need to do is plan how to draw his attention to you.'

'It can be a little difficult to command attention when surrounded by lunatics.'

'Oh, no, but that's perfect. There he is with all those people around him and who is that still, pale figure so dignified amidst it all? Why, it's the doctor's lovely daughter.'

'Don't,' Hannah blushed. 'I do need to do something, though. I think he's short-sighted. He doesn't seem to notice much and looks very closely at certain things.'

'Maybe that's being a poet: the distracted air.'

'Maybe. I don't think so, though. Sometimes he wears a monocle.'

'What we need to do,' Annabella said brightly, 'is arrange it so that I can see him, or meet him. I think that will help my assessment.'

Hannah looked at her smiling, excited friend and thought over the alarming idea. But before she could respond, Mademoiselle Leclair bustled in. The drawing—which Annabella briefly held up and which looked disappointingly accurate—was put aside.

'Bonjour, les filles,' Mademoiselle Leclair greeted them.

'Bonjour, Mademoiselle,' they both replied and opened their grammars.

*　　　*　　　*

William Stockdale the attendant was a taller man than the doctor, but he had to walk quickly to keep up with his master as they headed towards Leopard's Hill Lodge and the severe cases. Fulton Allen, the doctor's son, occasionally had to run to keep up. This was a general condition for Fulton, only just sixteen. His triumph, unknown to him, was not many months away. Before long he would be running the whole establishment alone. Presently he felt himself struggling, as always, in the turbulent wake of his father's surging energy. He strove to keep pace, to gain his father's mastery, to know what he knew, which, unfortunately for Fulton, was always expanding. This determination to match his father's stride and certainty felt particularly urgent when visiting the Lodge because it terrified him. Fairmead House was full of gentle disorder, idiocy and convalescence, even some, like Charles Seymour, who were not ill at all. Leopard's Hill Lodge was full of real madness, of agony, people lost to themselves. They were fierce and unpredictable. They smelled rank. They were obscene. They made sudden noises. Their suffering was bottomless. It was an abyss of contorted humanity, a circle of hell. All of Fulton's nightmares were set there as were his sexual dreams, which he also classified as nightmares no matter what the evidence of his sheets. Even the building looked mad: plain, square and tight, with regular small barred windows that emitted shrieks.

They marched towards it now, the forest a corridor of flickering light and shade.

Stockdale explained the case. 'He hasn't evacuated for three weeks now, I believe.'

'Suppression of evacuation will only render his mania worse. It's a cause. And the delusion hasn't left him?'

'What is his delusion?' Fulton asked.

Stockdale laughed. 'That if he does evacuate, he will poison the water, destroy the forest, and that it will permeate down and everyone in London will be killed.'

'Let's hope he's mistaken,' Fulton joked.

'Fulton,' Allen reproved. 'You cannot be facetious, certainly not with the patient. Madness has no sense of humour. How many people are there now? We'll need four at least to restrain him while I administer the clyster.'

'I can help,' Fulton offered meekly, angry at his father's humourless reproof.

'You can hold his head, maybe an arm. If you try to take a leg he'll kick you across the room. Unfortunately, he's a powerful and large man.'

That smell was there when they went through the door, just as Fulton had remembered, but always stronger, more shocking than he could anticipate. There were noises, but only two patients were in the large central space overlooked by the balcony and other rooms. The others were shut away. One of the loose ones stood still and rubbed a patch of scalp already rubbed bald. The other, a woman, ran towards them, staring at Stockdale, and began lifting her soiled dress. Fulton stared, horrified, but unable to look away. Before she'd revealed more than her dirty, folded knees, Stockdale took her arms firmly and tugged down her dress. 'She shouldn't be allowed to mix with men if she's subject to this . . .' Allen said.

Saunders, the attendant who'd opened the door to them, apologised. 'She hasn't behaved that poorly. I think it's you, doctor, or you, William.

Perhaps she expects an examination.'

The woman writhed, growing quieter in Stockdale's grasp. 'Don't want to do that,' she muttered. 'Don't want to do that.'

'That's quite right,' Allen told her. 'You don't.'

'Just let her go,' Saunders said. 'She'll be fine now, little outburst over.'

Saunders was short and strong and cheerful with blunt, capable hands that Fulton stared at. His fingertips were wide, the nails thick and yellow; his thumbs were jointed at two right angles, turning parallel to the palms. His eyes were bright among pleats of aged skin. Beneath one eyebrow hung two small growths, smaller than berries. He seemed to take his work easily. He smiled and hummed as he handled his charges, who were frantic with fear and pain. 'At eleven-thirty,' Saunders said, 'we'll let a few more out to exercise. These two have had bad nights is why they're out having a breather. But we'll address Mr Francombe first. I've two lads up by his door, plucking up courage.'

'Very good. Shall we go up?'

Saunders led the way up the stairs to the cells behind the balcony. From there Fulton looked down on the two freed patients, shuffling, drowsy as smoked bees.

'Morning, gentlemen,' Allen greeted the waiting attendants.

They replied and stepped away from the door. Allen looked through the grille at the big man sat leaning against a wall, grey-faced, holding his hard belly.

'Good morning, Mr Francombe,' Allen shouted through the door.

Dull eyes looked back at him, looked away.

29

Matthew Allen turned to his men. 'Very good. You four, I want you to get in, seize hold of him, and get him out of there. It will be best if he's in a bath, or on one of the tables, when I force the evacuation. Fulton, you stay here. Stockdale, Saunders, you take the legs. You other two, grab his arms. Do we all know what we're doing?'

'Yes, doctor,' Saunders answered. The others nodded.

'Very good. In you go.'

Saunders unlocked the door, lifted the latch. 'Ready?' he asked, and then the four of them strode in.

Fulton stood behind his father's shoulder and watched the struggle. Mr Francombe, after a volley of oaths, began roaring and bleating as he fought. His effort of violence was extraordinary. Saunders and Stockdale were flung back and forth as he kicked. The other two twisted and wrestled with his arms. He raised himself up off the ground between them, then sank down pulling his four limbs together so that the attendants bumped each other. From his face hung wisps of drool. He tried biting one of the men holding his arms. The attendant had to release the other arm and push back on Mr Francombe's forehead as hard as he could.

'Fulton, if you want to take part,' Allen said, in a surprisingly weary voice, 'you might usefully go in now. Go in behind him and get hold of his head. Get hold of his ears.'

'Really?'

'Fine. Hold this.' Allen handed his son his bag and went in himself. Fulton, shamed, followed him in.

30

Allen did as he'd instructed Fulton, circled quickly behind the five panting men, squatted down and tried to get a firm grip of Francombe's head. He thrashed so hard, though, and greasy hair covered his ears. Allen tried just pushing it down against the floor for a moment and saw the throat curdling with rage, the reddened knob of his Adam's apple and thick veins. He placed his knee on Francombe's forehead, pressed down with his body weight, scraped the hair away and got hold of the slimy gristle of his ears.

Slowly Francombe began to relent, throbbing, but as they lifted him to carry him out, he began to thrash again, and the five of them staggered as on a stormy deck.

When finally they had him tethered to a table, Francombe was whimpering with rage and humiliation. His trousers and underthings had been removed. Matthew Allen, with trembling hands, wiped the sweat from his face.

'Now, Mr Francombe. You know that what you fear is not rational, is not true. We each of us must void our waste. We each of us do void our wastes, and forests do not die. Cities are not poisoned.'

'Oh, aren't they?' Francombe snapped back. 'Aren't they?'

'Your waste is no more noxious than anyone else's. It is not sin, you know. It isn't. It's nothing you've done. It is the by-product of alimentation. Do you understand? It is waste food.'

Francombe was quiet, then strained all at once at his straps. They creaked as he pulled, exhaling slowly through his widely spaced teeth. Fulton wondered if they would definitely hold.

'Oh, let's just get on with it,' Allen muttered. He

31

had the clyster ready, in one hand the pipe, in the other the bag full of warm salted water. 'Fulton, you don't have to watch, you know. It won't be pleasant.'

Fulton vacillated only briefly. 'I hadn't been expecting pleasantness,' he said. 'And one day I'll have to face these procedures.'

'Very good. If you are to stay, perhaps you could massage the abdomen for me.'

Allen then bent and inserted the nozzle into the dark, crimped entrance of Mr Francombe's rectum. He pushed it several inches in, apparently oblivious to the manhood that flopped from side to side within a foot of his face as he did so.

Allen started squeezing in the fluid. 'Now, pressure from the top of the abdomen down, please. And hard.'

Fulton did as he was told, pushing against what he took to be the compacted shit inside Mr Francombe. The attendants stood apart, arms folded, and chatted.

Warm clear liquid washed out of Mr Francombe. 'Harder, please,' Allen called over the man's moans. 'And you too, Mr Francombe. You can push.'

Mr Francombe struggled to resist, but the warm water, the pushing on his belly, the pain, all made it very difficult not to let go. Before too long Dr Allen was rewarded with numerous stuttering farts followed by the emergence of a tiny hard stool, folded like a sea shell. 'Very good.' He squeezed in more water.

'Whore,' Mr Francombe said. 'Bugger. Dirty bugger. Shit licker.'

Another small turd emerged, then a massive fart,

then another. They were getting larger, almost the size of sheep's droppings. 'Good, Fulton.'

'Dirty bugger! Ow!'

Francombe now wept with disappointment as an astonishing quantity of shit bloomed from him across the table. Allen stayed there, squeezing still on the clyster, despite the spoiling of his shoes by falling clumps.

'Hoo, hoo,' exclaimed Saunders, flapping at the air in front of his face. 'And you call us dirty buggers.'

'Thank you, Mr Saunders,' Allen chastised. 'I expect Mr Francombe will be very upset by this experience. Mr Stockdale, I suggest you take him out to the clearing in the forest afterwards and let him vent a while. Perhaps, Mr Saunders, you could go with him.'

'Certainly, doctor.'

'I'll apply leeches to his feet later when you get back and we can all look forward to a less sanguine, restored Mr Francombe.'

'Very good, doctor.'

With his shoes scraped roughly clean, the ordure worked from under his fingernails with the blade of a penknife, Matthew Allen walked out of Leopard's Hill Lodge. Fulton carried his bag for him. They returned to the gentle distresses and confusions of Fairmead House. Allen was happy to return, but only relatively. He was tired, very tired of the mad and their squalor, and the stubborn resistance to cure of the majority. His mind strained for an idea of something else to do, some expansion.

Crossing the lawn where George Laidlaw stood in a fever of mental arithmetic, where one idiot

33

chased another but stopped at the sight of the approaching doctor, and the patients with the axe were again filling the barrow, John Clare approached.

'John, John, how are you feeling today?'

'Perfectly well, doctor, perfectly well. And that's just it, you see.'

'Is it now?'

'I was wondering, you see, given how trustworthy I have been and so forth, if I might be allowed to join those who have a pass key.'

'To ramble and rhyme?' Of course, John Clare. There was a thought.

John winced at that, then nodded. 'To walk. To botanise and so forth.'

'You are still writing poems, aren't you?' Allen asked. 'Those I read a little while ago I thought effusions of great beauty. And your reputation is surely not sunk to oblivion. When did you last seek publication?'

'Such effusions, as you call them, rural effusions, are no longer to the public's taste.'

'Perhaps you would allow me to assay for you? I'd be happy to write to a few literary connections of mine for magazine publication.'

'I wouldn't expect anything to come of it,' said Clare, wary of the painful heat of hope that could flare inside him.

'I'll take it upon myself. It won't be a trouble to you.'

'I suppose there's no harm . . .'

'Excellent. Why not? Productions such as yours should not be confined to a dusty drawer in a hospital. I shall get you that key, if you'll follow me.'

'Thank you, doctor.'

*   *   *

John set off immediately with the key in his hand. Peter Wilkins smiled at John with his watery eyes and reached for his own key, but John lifted up his. Peter Wilkins straightened. 'Oh,' he said. 'You've a key. Good to see, John, good to see.'

John was embarrassed at this congratulation, but warmed at it anyway. He tried to mask its effect, responding with a bluff, countryish, 'And the weather's fair.'

'You have a good walk, now,' the old man said after him. 'It lifts me up to see it.'

John raised a hand in farewell as he struck out along the path, past the familiar forms of the nearby trees, out to the strangers that grew hidden for miles around. Ferns, dying back with the season, stood frazzled between them. There was no song, just a few notes seeping from overhead as he passed and the quiet birds warned each other. A blackbird, frisking through the fallen leaves, bounced up away from his feet, settled on a low branch and twittered alarm, staring fiercely back at him.

John studied the bird's daffodil-yellow beak, sharp as tweezers, its neat handsome black head, and absorbed the stare from its glinting round eye. Doing so he heard a human shout. He walked on, away from the noise, but was deceived by the forest's maze of echoes and came right upon one of the patients barefoot on moss and leaves, his shoes discarded, sweating and gesticulating. When he saw John he started towards him, his face raw with rage, but two attendants were with him. One sprang up from a log on which they were playing with a pack of old, bent cards, and raised his arms. The lunatic pretended not to see him, but stopped where he was.

'Move on there,' the attendant told John. It was Stockdale. 'Move on. No harm done. Had a bit of a morning, that one. Don't fret yourself.' The other attendant, whom John didn't quite recognise, smiled through his pipe smoke.

John hurried on, removing his hat, wiping out the brim dampened by sudden fear, and setting it firmly back on his head.

After some yards, he lifted his gaze from the loosely matted leaves, the prickly star-shapes of beech-nut shells, and the roots that ribbed the path. He looked up again and saw the glaring, hooked darkness of holly bushes, the long whips and shabby leaves of brambles beneath them. He picked a blackberry and ate it: so tart it made his palate itch.

He walked on. He found a rotting trunk covered in fungus, rippling lines of livid yellow Jew's ears eating away at the softened wood. Listening to what? He looked at them closely, their whorls, the wash of colour across them that went in waves or rings, pinkish towards the outer edge.

And there at one end of the log was scattered evidence that it was used as a thrush's anvil. On the flattest part of the trunk a bird had brought snails and with them in its beak, whipping its neck back and forth, had smashed them open. Smithereens of spiral shell, some with a frail foam of mucus still on them, made a constellation that John swirled with his fingertip.

But he couldn't touch Mary, he remembered—
the sweetest of his two wives, the lost child who
loved him, so near in his thoughts he could reach
out and touch her. 'Mary,' he crooned to himself.
Time's walls were the strangest prison. He couldn't
touch them or bloody his head against them, but
they surrounded him without a gap, and kept him
from his loves, from home, lost in a wood miles
away from them. He stood up. 'Mary,' he said. 'O
Mary. O Mary. O Mary sing thy songs to me.' He
dug in his pockets: his pipe, a pebble, a square of
paper and bit of old pencil. He sat down again,
removed his hat, flattened the paper over its crown
and wrote,

> O Mary sing thy songs to me
> Of love & beauty's melody
> My sorrows sink beneath distress . . .

After a spell there he had a new poem written on
both sides of the paper, and then across for lack of
room. He sat feeling whole for a moment, his mind
serene and extensive, running through the poem,
humming it. The wood surrounded him, its arms
upraised, meeting the light. A fine rain had started
to stutter onto branches and leaves.

Another poem, among thousands. It was
comfortable to have them come singly, not
streaming out in a fever. His flash company that
had been the ruin of him quite. He remembered
with a clench of his bowels his friends in the village
avoiding him so as not to find themselves in a
poem they couldn't read and that brought the
visiting strangers. *Is it true, as I have heard, that you
rustics perform the conjugal act in your pig sties?*

Still, it would please Dr Allen, he reflected. Another ornament to his thoroughly respectable establishment of lunatics.

John walked on, passing charcoal burners sitting inside their huts, ancient things of poles walled with cut turf, old as any dwelling probably. They had to spend days out there, making sure the fires didn't catch, but slowly ate down to coal the wood piled under covers. The smoke that rose was sweet, much sweeter than at the lime kilns where John had worked off and on. He saw them look up and stare out of their darkness and risked a greeting doffing of his hat, but they didn't move.

Then, half a mile away, in a clearing there were vardas, painted caravans, tethered horses, and children, and a smoking fire. A little terrier caught the scent of John and stood with its four feet planted, leaning towards him, as if in italics, to bark. An old woman seated near the fire, a blanket around her shoulders, looked up. John didn't move or say anything.

'Good day to you,' she said.

'Good day,' John answered, and then to let her know he knew them, was a friend, said, 'Cushti hatchintan.'

She raised her eyebrows at that. 'It is. It is a good spot. You rokkers Romany then, do you?'

'Somewhat, I do. I was often with the gypsies near my hatchintan, in Northamptonshire. We had many long nights. They taught me to fiddle their tunes and such. Abraham Smith, and Phoebe. You know them?'

'We're Smiths here, but I don't know your crew. I haven't been into that county, or had them here. This is a good spot,' she raised an arm to gesture at

38

it. 'Plenty of land and no one pushing you off it. And the forest creatures, lots of hotchiwitchis to eat in winter. This is one commons that don't seem to be getting ate up.'

John shook his head and answered as one weary elder to another. 'It's criminal what is nominated law now. Theft only, taking the common land from the people. I remember when they came to our village with their telescopes to measure and fence and parcel out. The gypsies then were driven out. The poor also.'

One of the children ran over to the old lady and whispered in her ear, watching John. The others stood apart like cats, eyes among the branches. The terrier that had warned of John's coming now jogged over to join the children's conspiracy.

The old woman spoke. 'He thinks you might be a forest constable or a gamekeeper who might not be keen on us here.'

Wanting very much to stay in this comfortable loose nest of a place, with the free people, John declared himself. 'I'm homeless myself, sleeping nearby. And often I've been arrested by gamekeepers.' This was true: he'd often been mistaken for a poacher as he skulked and wrote his poems, a man with no reason to be in that place but being there.

'What's your name?'

'John. John Clare.'

'Well, I'm Judith Smith. I take you as an acceptable man, John Clare, pale and lorn, albeit well fed, whoever you are. I smell the wrong in men, crosswise intentions, and I don't smell that in you, with your foolish open face. I'm known for my duckering, and my predictions have proved most accurate, most accurate.'

'I know many ballads. I can sing, if you like.'

Judith Smith laughed and pulled a twig from the fire to light her pipe. 'Later, if you like when the others get back. Quick at making friends, ain't I? The chavvies are fearful, but they'll simmer down.'

John looked round at the children, four or five of them keeping their distance, as the one who'd whispered to her sprinted back to them.

'Chavvies ought to be fearful,' John said. 'It might save them now and again.'

'It's possible. Will you sit, then? You can keep the yog going till we've something to cook. That's why they's worrying. Fellers have gone off to get something to eat, you see, and they don't want it ruined.'

'Quite right,' John said.

So John sat beside her and poked the fire, turning its sticks to keep it burning while the chavvies gradually lost their fear and ran over to sprinkle dry leaves on, waiting for the ones that caught and lifted on wandering, pirouetting flights that drifted at times excitingly towards them. The old woman offered John a wooden pipe to smoke, its stem dented with yellow tooth marks, but he showed her his own. He drew whistling sour air through it to check it would draw, then filled it from a twist of tobacco she had. That wrapper of old newspaper was probably the only bit of printed matter in the place and John smiled to see it put to good use, its smudged words unread, its sharp voices sounding in nobody's mind. He lit his pipe with a burning twig. They talked about the weather and the plants. Long silences between thoughts were filled with the sound of the fire and the ceaseless sound of wind through the branches, bird flights, scurryings.

Younger women emerged from the caravans— they must have been hiding there the whole time— and John made himself known to them. They seemed less certain of his presence than Judith Smith, offering the bare bones of greetings as they went about their business, rinsing pots, gathering more wood for the fire, smacking dirt from the chavvies' clothes. John liked the brisk, free, tumbled life around him and watched it affectionately as the fire grew ruddier against the weakening light.

The men's voices returned a few minutes before they did. By then the fire had been enlarged and pots arranged. As the voices approached, the children stopped burying each other in leaves and even pushed their hair back out of their faces. The dog, frantic, barked and ran in tight circles to bark again. It ran off to meet the men and returned ahead of the party with a few rangy lurchers and a blurring number of other terriers.

When John saw the men and the deer slung between two of them, covered in a blanket but still obvious, he knew what all the caginess had been about. He stood up immediately to introduce himself. 'I'm John Clare, a traveller, and always a friend of the gypsies. I bring cordial greetings from Abraham and Phoebe Smith of Northamptonshire.'

'He's a good fellow,' Judith attested. 'Knows the plants and cures as well as we do. He must've been long with those Smiths because he knows all our names for them.'

The foremost man made a decision as quick as

41

Judith's had been. He answered with the formality of a man speaking for his tribe. 'S'long as you are no friend of the gamekeepers and don't fall to talking with them you're welcome among us, John Clare. My name is Ezekiel.'

So John was let stay and watched the men, who didn't seem in any way encumbered by thoughts of transportation and a life of whippings at Botany Bay as they dismantled the deer.

He watched with great pleasure the skill of the men, their knives quick as fish. They said nothing, only the work made noises, knockings on joints, wet peelings, the twisting crunch of a part disconnected.

First, a trench was dug to receive and hide the blood and the deer was hung from a branch upside down above it. With sharpened knives they slit it quickly down the middle and found the first stomach. Very carefully one man cut either side of it, and knotted the slippery tubes to keep the gut acid from the meat. This made something like a straw-stuffed cushion, filled with undigested herbage.

Then the forelimbs were cut through to the precise white joints and removed. After loosening work with a knife, the skin was pulled from the deer. It peeled away cleanly with a moist sucking sound, leaving dark meat and bones beneath a sheeny blue underskin. As they did all this, the men had to kick at the dogs that were crowding round the trench to lap at blood.

The gullet was separated and the weasand was drawn from the windpipe. They cleared the chest of its entrails. The heart and lungs were snicked out and placed in a bowl, then the long rippled ropes of the intestines were hauled out and dropped into the trench. Working from the back, the chuck, saddle and loin portions were removed from the ribcage and spine in one piece, both sides together like a bloody book the size of a church Bible. They were then cut into pieces, some of which were sliced and spitted immediately over the fire. Other parts were taken away by the women. Then the neck was stripped of meat. The deer looked odd now with its whole furred head and antlers hanging down, its skeleton neck and body, and its breeches of flesh still on. Those too were now removed, divided, and packed. The ribs were sawn through, and all of them were split and set over the fire. The deer now was clean. Its skeleton faintly glowed in the dusk, its sorrowful head merged with the shadows. Another pit was dug and the skeleton was placed inside it, curled around like a foetus. The earth was replaced, leaves and twigs dragged over to hide the spot.

The dogs jostled round the other trench in a cloud of flies. John could hear the knocking of their empty jaws and short huffing breaths. With the smell of the venison rising in the smoke, John's own hunger became acute and his guts let out a long crooning grumble like a pigeon's note. Beer was poured and drunk and soon the air was splashy with talk and voices. John didn't join in very much, but listened to the flow and switch of it, hearing Romany words he'd almost forgotten he knew.

Handed his first rib, John was told, 'Blood on your hands, my friend. You're our accomplice now.' The meat was delicious, charred muscle to tear at and smooth soft fat. There was no harm in eating the deer, to John's mind: they kept

43

themselves; there were many in the forest. They flowed unnumbered through the shadows.

Afterwards there was more drink and music while bats, in their last flights of the year, flickered overhead. John proved his claim to know their music when he accepted a fiddle from them. He played Northamptonshire tunes and gypsy tunes. He played one that circled like a merry-go-round and lifted them all smiling on its refrain. He played a tune that reached out and up, branching into the trees. He played a tune that was flat and lonely as the fens, cold as winter mist. He played one for Mary. After he'd played, there was singing, John listened to the strong joined voices, adding his own notes of harmony, and his mind's eye swept back to see them all in the middle of the darkened forest, in the circle of firelight, the bloody-muzzled dogs lying outstretched beside their hard-packed bellies. The people made a well of song; it surged up from eternity into that moment, a source. He lay back, really overwhelmed, and saw stars through the almost bare branches. He closed his eyes and lay there in the middle of the world, denied his wives, his home, but accompanied and peaceful.

Eventually the singing stopped and a little while after that he felt a blanket placed over him. He opened his eyes to see the rosy fire still breathing at the heart of white sticks. An owl cried its dry, hoarse cry and the bats still scattered their tiny beads of sound around him. He loved lying in its lap, the continuing forest, the way the roots ate the rot of leaves, and it circled on. To please himself, to decorate his path into sleep, he passed through his mind an inventory of its creatures. He saw the trees, beech, oak, hornbeam, lime, holly, hazel, and

44

the berries, the different mushrooms, ferns, moss, lichens. He saw the rapid, low foxes, the tremulous deer, lone wild cats, tough, trundling badgers, the different mice, the bats, the day animals and night animals. He saw the snails, the frogs, the moths that looked like bark and the large, ghost-winged moths, the butterflies: orange tips, whites, fritillaries, the ragged-winged commas. He recounted the bees, the wasps. He thought of all the birds, the drumming woodpeckers and laughing green woodpeckers, the stripe of the nuthatch, the hook-faced sparrowhawks, the blackbirds and the tree creeper flinching up the trunks of trees. He saw the blue tits flicking between branches, the white flash of the jay's rump as it flew away, the pigeons sitting calmly separate, together in a tree. He saw the fierce, sweet-voiced robin. He saw the sparrows.

And just before he fell asleep, he saw himself, his head whole, his body stripped down to a damp skeleton, placed gently, curled around, in a hole in the earth.

*　　　*　　　*

John woke with one side of his face tingling. He opened his eyes and found that it wasn't the numbness, but a light rain pattering down onto him; with almost inaudible thumps it fell also into the soft ashes of the exhausted fire. Beyond that, wet trees gleamed.

He pulled the blanket up over his face and soon his breath made a warm, sleepy pocket under the coarse wool.

John woke again to people moving, dogs

stretching. Judith, puffing with bellows into a new fire, smiled.

'I have to go,' he said.

'To that place away up the road?' she asked. He nodded. He had suspected that she would have guessed. 'Don't see why you have to be there myself,' she said. 'Anyone who plays the fiddle like that.'

'Thank you.' He stood, shook out and folded his blanket, then, not wanting to give her anything to do by handing it to her, placed it back on the ground where he'd slept.

'We'll be here the winter most likely, so if you want to come back . . .'

'Thank you,' he said again. 'I will, if I can.' He raised his voice to address anyone near. 'Thank you. I have to go now.'

'After a bit of food,' Judith suggested.

'Thanks, I'm full enough for a while.'

John hurried away or tried to. First he had to shake hands with all the children who'd run to make a ring around him.

The sun was still low and he reckoned it to be early, perhaps early enough to slip back in unnoticed. The charcoal burners weren't at their hut. He passed a birdcatcher with two cages swinging from his pole, on his way to London where song was needed. The morning's catch of finches flew against the narrow bars. The catcher tilted his hat. John did the same and when he'd passed him shook his head at the gross symbol, refusing the easy poem he was offered.

He was back at the gate before Peter Wilkins. With his own key, he let himself back in. He trudged up the path to Fairmead House and was almost in when Matthew Allen stepped out.

He saw John—he couldn't not, they were barely three feet apart—and looked disappointed.

'John, this is very bad,' he began and John felt anger suddenly buckle inside him, with no possible release. He had done wrong and he knew it and had now to submit to being reprimanded like a child. He tried answering like a child.

'I got lost.'

'Did you?'

'In the dark. I walked too far.'

Matthew Allen looked at him, sucked at his moustache. John looked back, then down. There was a moment of stalemate before Allen said, 'It absolutely must not happen again. Can you assure me of that?'

'I won't walk that far, doctor. And I'll pay more mind to where I am. I was composing was maybe part of the trouble.'

'Ah, yes, John. After our conversation I collected a few poems from your room. To send to editors.' Matthew Allen blinked a few times, perhaps not quite sure of the decency of this invasion.

John saw this, but didn't mind; he welcomed the chance to even the advantage. 'Oh, did you?' he said casually to heat any embarrassment there might be in the doctor. 'As I was saying,' John went on, 'I was composing yesterday. A poem to my wife, Mary. It's fine I think. I can write it up for you fair to go with the others you took.'

Matthew Allen shook his head. 'John, we've talked about this. You know that Mary is not your wife. She was your childhood sweetheart. A child, John, a girl of what nine or ten? Patty is your wife, and I know she finds this fixed idea of yours most

47

distressing.'

'No,' John said. 'No, I am well acquainted with the truth.' He knew also that what was law and what was natural were not the same thing. 'Mary is my wife. And so's Patty. Just because a thing hasn't happened before doesn't mean it can't. And anyway it has occurred, in the Bible.'

*   *   *

Hannah had offered to take Abigail for a walk. As they'd set out, she'd confused the child by turning her from the usual route, on this occasion, towards Beach Hill House.

Abigail preferred walking with her mother, who took more of an interest in what she picked up, pretty stones or feathers. Hannah's attention was elsewhere, across and away somewhere, not down with Abigail, and she walked too quickly. Abigail caught her sleeve and leaned her whole weight back over her heels to slow her sister, but she was pulled forward into a trot.

'I hope you're planning to behave,' Hannah said, 'or I shall take you straight back.'

Hannah's angrily swishing legs marched ahead. Abigail chased after, then her sister suddenly stopped.

'Why have we stopped?' she asked. 'Stopped the wrong way?'

'Shh, Abi. I'm thinking.'

'But what are you thinking?'

'Shh.'

Hannah stood and looked at the house where he was living, set behind its own large pond and lawn. Formerly of no significance, this place was now

48

charged and thrilling as a beehive. She stood up on her tiptoes to see more. Taking a few paces up like a ballet dancer to bring a hidden corner of the garden into view, she saw him. It must have been him. Such a tall man, his back turned to her, standing still, in a thick cloud of his own manufacture, wearing that cape. She stood as still as she could, her heartbeats strong enough to unsteady her, absolutely at the edge of her life. Something had to happen soon. It had to.

Abigail, bored and frustrated, ran into her with both arms outstretched and shoved at her bottom.

'Don't,' Hannah span round and hissed. She caught hold of Abigail's hand and tugged the child towards her. Abigail saw her sister's face, bright with a flush of anger, swooping towards her. Her lips were trembling. She looked very ugly like that. Abigail tried to free herself from Hannah's grasp, but Hannah shook her arm hard, standing up and looking away again.

Uncertainly postured between cringing out of sight and standing up tall to see, Hannah tried to ascertain whether Alfred Tennyson had heard the commotion. As she did so she felt the warm wetness of Abigail's small mouth close around her wrist and her little cat's teeth bite in. She couldn't help it, she cried out and definitely now Tennyson had heard. She bobbed up and saw his large shape turning. She ducked and ran, dragging a wailing Abigail after her. When they returned and had calmed down she could bribe the child with a chip of sugar not to tell.

*   *   *

49

Alfred Tennyson did not try to comfort or even make contact with his brother, Septimus, sitting beside him. When he had tried, the little hits of familial concern seemed to hurt him, and he'd shrink away, raising a hand and trying, horribly, to smile. Instead, Tennyson stretched his long legs in front of him in a casual manner he permitted himself while the patients were still arriving but would be corrected when the evening prayers began.

He looked vaguely towards Mrs Allen who played the organ, actually rather well. Her pale daughter, so thin and restless she flickered in his field of blurred vision, turned the pages. He closed his eyes and listened to the sound. It rose in regular crests of force as the treadle pump cycled air through the pipes and Tennyson saw the ridged sound abstractly, thought of the sea, of Mablethorpe, the heavy, low waves and hardened undulations of the sand after the tide had withdrawn. Words began. *Waves. Rocks. Lashed.* Or *felt. Waters that feel the scraping rocks, scourging rocks. Waters that feel the scourging rocks as they rush. That feel the sharp rocks as they rush.*

Margaret watched the other poor souls take their seats to pray and again did not know what to think. She suspected that nothing there could be real, that when the doctor preached his watery sermons the Presence would swerve away, offended. She would. But then she lacked compassion, hating human weakness, so when they prayed was she the only one cut off, bogged down in sin, while the others prayed purely and were heard? God pitied them. And why pity her who was pitiless? She'd never liked the complications of joined prayer, all

50

the human interference and distraction. She could only find her way alone. And in that solitude a part of her suspected she was lost, cut off, adrift.

They all started singing now, all upright. John Clare stood and added his voice to the compound of mad voices without much fervour. Seated beside the fire, he was distracted by its blustering heat. The attendants sang evenly, watchfully. One of the idiots sang very loudly but Simon beside him sang without noise, just opening and closing his lips while he rubbed at his left eye. Clara, the witch, never sang. She stared around and tried, when people looked back at her, to laugh to herself.

After they'd all stumbled down the short step of the two notes for 'Amen', Dr Allen patted them back into their seats with gently flapping hands and began this evening's sermon.

This was the seventh of his addresses on the Beatitudes and he cleared his throat before pronouncing, 'Blessed are the peacemakers for they shall be called the children of God.' He felt splendidly paternal and sincere when he gave his sermons, looking out over his flock of patients, their stricken eyes latched onto him. He sensed his wife seated behind him at the organ, saw three of his children seated before him. Fulton had his hair combed differently, somehow, perhaps in the opposite direction to usual, and this made him seem independently attentive, his own man, making his own decisions, and voluntarily there, voluntarily following his father into medicine. Dora, the quietest of his children, well matched with her betrothed, appeared to be trying to stop Abigail kicking her legs under the seat. Among the others, George Laidlaw's gaze was particularly direct. He waited each day for the evening prayers; they brought him his only short hours of relief from the terrors of the National Debt for which his mind told him he was solely responsible.

Dr Allen enumerated several categories of peacemakers, among them those who bring an end to wars and discord. But there were other kinds of peacemakers, those who bring an end to the bitter strife of internal discord. Margaret knew that he meant himself and scorned his weakness for saying it. She almost pitied him the affliction of his vanity. Friends are such peacemakers, he went on, who bring peace through calm and the nourishing atmosphere of affection. It is not only those we know as peacemakers—curates, ambassadors, doctors—who bring these resolutions, then, but all of us, in our fellowship.

John knew what would bring him peace: his wives, Mary and Patty. Peace would have been lying beneath an oak with them on either side in a sweet, heavy smell of grass, the sun warm on them, thick curds of summer cloud moving slowly over. He turned from the sight of Matthew Allen rocking up onto his toes with each commonplace preacher's phrase that pleased him, and stared into the fire. His thoughts began picking up uncomfortable speed as he looked and realised that those were particular logs being consumed, logs from particular trees burning with particular flames in that exact place at that specific hour and it would only ever occur once in the history of the world and that was now. Birds had landed on them, particular birds, and creatures had crawled across them, light had revolved around them, winds swayed them, unique clouds passed over them, and they would be ashes in the morning. There was so little time. He needed to be free with his wives in each living day, not consuming them here. Forked or foliate, the flames themselves were as singular as the trees, eternal and vanishing in quick snaps.

Hannah ignored her father's words, looked past the tails of his coat, his hands floating from the sides of the lectern to pat his pages square, to where the Tennysons were sitting. Alfred Tennyson's face was pensive, brooding—how else would it be?—but she couldn't keep her eyes on him. To his right, his brother's face seemed as set as a death mask, his eyes lightly closed, but down his cheeks ran tears. Eventually she saw him part his sore lips to inhale. Without opening his eyes he dried his cheeks with a handkerchief. As he then wavered to his feet with the rest, Hannah realised it was time to sing again.

Tennyson stood and sang as all of the afflicted opened their valves to God. The sermon had been decent, in his estimation, clearer and more clearly delivered than those of his own deceased father, more generously and compassionately addressed to his congregation. Afterwards, as the patients handed their hymnals to the attendants and began to leave, and Septimus hobbled away, Tennyson approached the doctor to offer his compliments. Hannah saw him do this and hurried to her father's side.

Tennyson took Allen's hand and shook it. 'I thought that sermon fine,' he said.

'I'm pleased at that,' Allen replied.

'It was excellent,' Hannah chipped in.

Allen turned with some surprise at this interjection from his unusually interested

53

daughter, smiled indulgently and grasped her shoulder. Hannah stiffened at this contact and looked down, feeling painfully thwarted by only being able to appear as a child to them. But instantly she decided that to take the part of a pretty and devoted daughter was her most winning option, so again she surprised Allen by patting the back of his hand in response.

As this family interchange was happening, Tennyson was distracted by the approach of another man. He smiled, Tennyson saw as he neared, and his head lightly trembled. He took the doctor's hand in both of his own and shook it. 'Thank you,' he said, 'thank you again.' After he had turned away, Allen explained to Tennyson who he was, how he suffered from the National Debt, and how these prayers were his only respite. Tennyson watched the man's retreating back, his gait tightening the further away he was from this remarkably effective doctor.

Winter

Margaret stood in the dead of the world and looked down at the stopped fish under their dirty window of ice. In the black forks of the trees hard snow was pock-marked by later rain. Crows, folded tightly into themselves, clasped branches that plunged in the wind. Voices of other patients reached her there, the sound dulled by the covered winter surfaces like the clapping of gloved hands.

She liked the pinch of absence, the hollow air, reminiscent of the real absence. She wanted to stay out there, to hang on her branch in the world until the cold had burned down to her bones. She could leave her whitened bones scattered on the snow and depart like light. Whitened bones. *A whited sepulchre.* The phrase came to her. Was it aimed at her? Is that why she'd thought of it? Habitually, she tested every bit of scripture that came to her for immediate significance. The whited sepulchre was the Pharisee, according to Him, who appears beautiful, but inside is full of *dead men's bones and all uncleanness*. But isn't that every human creature? And what if the uncleanness had been her husband's, had been daubed on her, slapped on, smeared across her face? What use was always asking questions? As though thought was in any way helpful. Nothing could be argued into being. Whatever was, was. The only useful thing was to be unclouded by thoughts, to be in nothing. To be nothing. To be as empty as the cold. And to wait.

Again she was denied this. She heard the crunch of footsteps behind her and waited for them to diminish away, but they grew louder. She turned. Footprints ran everywhere across the buried lawn

57

like blue stitches. The sky was grey, darker than the ground: dreamlight: a steady stormlight. At the head of new lines of footprints were Clara the witch and Simon the idiot who dawdled after her, kicking up spurts of ice.

Margaret stared at Clara, at the large lips that didn't quite fit together, at the unpinned hair that draggled over her shoulders. Clara obviously thought of herself as sensual with a rolling walk, a flaunt in it, but she wasn't. Her figure was ordinary, her face unexceptional, blander and healthier than her mind. 'Good morning, Mary,' she smiled. Calling Margaret Mary was a spiteful joke of hers. Margaret said nothing. 'Not going to say anything, are you?' Margaret stared. 'Devils eaten your words?' Scratching his thighs through his pockets, the idiot asked, 'What devils?'

'I told you before.'

Margaret looked at them for a moment more, then turned back to the pond.

Their voices said more words, finally the hard separate ones of insult. But they were mistaken in thinking they could disturb Margaret's concentration.

An hour or so later she heard more footsteps coming towards her. This time hands landed on her shoulders. She was pivoted around to find herself looking into the doctor's face. He said, 'Margaret, you're freezing. How long have you been out here?' He chafed her hands between his. 'You're shivering.' She was—that flashing and shuddering was shivering. 'Come inside.' With an arm across the bones of her shoulders, he shepherded her into Fairmead House and a fire.

In its thick, disappointing heat she gradually

58

stopped shaking. Hot tea was forced into her, causing pain to the chilled stones of her teeth. The liquid billowed inside her, swelled her. She closed her eyes, let the doctor's words bump like moths against her, and drifted into sleep.

*   *   *

Eliza Allen opened the door to someone whose face was familiar but unplaceable. The face had evidently been out in the cold for some time, the skin grey and granular. The man blew a fog of warm breath around his hands. He smiled.

'Do you not recognise me, Eliza?'

With the voice, the accent, she did. 'Of course I do. It's Oswald. Come in, come in. I had no idea you were in the area. Matthew hadn't mentioned to me . . .'

'Because he doesn't know. I thought I'd surprise you.'

'And you have. Come in. Do.'

Oswald stooped to pick up a bag. Presumably he was expecting to stay. When he was upright again a noise startled him. Eliza saw his body for a moment lose organisation. He half-crouched, knees bent, and raised a hand. His gaze locked with hers. 'One of the patients?' he whispered.

'No, no,' she reassured him. 'That was a dog barking, surely.'

'Of course.'

Inside, she relieved him of his coat and hat. By the fire his face flushed, his eyes reddened and filmed. He looked tired.

'Do sit down.' She indicated the chair.

He did so, crossing his legs and tucking his

59

clasped hands down the side of one thigh in his peculiar fashion, wearing his arms like a sash. By now he was very recognisable. 'I shall fetch tea. You must need it after your journey.'

'Most kind.'

She hurried out. Finding Dora in the second drawing room, she instructed her to put down whatever it was and go and tell her father that his brother had suddenly materialised. 'Father's in his study,' Dora replied.

'Then it won't take you a moment.'

Eliza returned with a tray of tea things just as her husband launched himself into the room.

'Oswald, I had no idea.'

'I didn't give you any idea,' his brother smiled. 'And I'm delighted to see you too.'

Matthew blended a smile and a frown to indicate fondly that the implication was foolish. 'I'm pleased to see you, too, of course. Your journey was comfortable?'

'Perfectly agreeable, at least so far as these things are. And I rounded it off with a pleasant walk from Woodford.'

'You walked up? Carrying your bag? You could have hired a cab, you know. Mr Mason is known around the station to take people.'

'Oh, no. Thrift, Horatio, thrift.'

Horatio? That meant *Hamlet*. Oswald was reminding Matthew of the cultured company he kept in York, that not only in London was there literary conversation to be had. Typical of him to arrive stealthily like this, unannounced, and full of messages about himself, all his little flags flying.

Matthew Allen, flustered, forgot the tongs and picked up a lump of sugar with his fingertips, dropping it with a small splash into his tea. 'It's a surprising time for you to visit,' he said, 'by which I mean for an apothecary. Are you not now besieged by the winter ailments?'

'Fortunately, yes,' Oswald laughed. 'But I have left the shop in good hands. I have an apprentice and two others at the moment.' More impressive news about himself. 'I keep my hours at the shop to a minimum now that I'm able, and so have more time for my benevolent activities and so forth.'

'Oh, very good.' Matthew gulped his tea.

'You could have been joined with me in that, had you not chosen another course.' Oswald smiled. 'But we needn't go into that.'

Matthew smiled. 'Ah, but I did choose another course.' He would not be drawn again into this conversation. Indeed he saw an opportunity for a moment's triumph and couldn't resist, relishing the plural he was able to deploy. 'I shall give you a tour of the buildings, my alternative course, later before we install you in a room.'

*   *   *

Dr Allen savoured his time at the lectern during evening prayers as a period when he was unopposed, central and secure. He chose to read his brother's expression—downcast eyes, thoughtfully lengthened lips—as simple absorption even though he knew he would not approve. Oswald's face instead insisted on his own distinct piety. He did not hesitate to begin his criticism after the service was concluded. With patients still ambling out and George Laidlaw having offered again his heartfelt thanks, at which Oswald smiled,

61

apparently bemused, he began: 'It's a long way from anything our father would recognise, Matthew.'

'It is indeed. As I suppose we are, or I am.'

'Hm.' Oswald nodded. 'Father would not have approved such Latitudinarianism.'

'Of course. But you see, needs must. I'm preaching for a very mixed congregation, and not only denominationally, if it comes to that.'

'He would maintain that there are differences between sects and that he'd brought us up in the true dogma. I mean to say, the point is simple. How can the truth be graspable by churches that we know to be in error?'

'Oswald, even if I wanted to I could not make this institution Sandemanian. For one thing, our little church would require a great deal of explanation to those whose intellectual faculties are in many cases already strained to breaking point. And the need for the congregation's unity of mind—it's hardly a practicable aim with a congregation of the insane and the idiot.'

'And indeed you yourself rarely managed it.'

'Indeed.' Matthew Allen looked down at his brother, some years older, some inches shorter, and still trying to rule in their father's place. 'I was excluded often enough. So there, you see,' he attempted to laugh. 'I was not a good enough Sandemanian to be worthy to attempt to create a community here.'

Oswald did not laugh. 'You were always too soft in spirit and too distracted by the world. It didn't suit you to be part of an isolated church, unknown to society, and lacking all ornament. You didn't like the poverty, the hardship . . .'

'Really, Oswald, must we discuss this? I thought we very much had some time ago. And I see enough hardship here among my patients, often without seeing to what end it serves.'

Oswald snorted. 'A different meaning of hardship, surely. I remember your disgust at father's funeral because of its simplicity. Yes, maybe simplicity is closer to my meaning.'

That was true enough. Matthew Allen remembered the scene with discomfort—the bare hills dotted all over with the little wet tubes of sheep turds, the animals' loud bleats carried to the mourners on the slanting wind, the ugly, parted ground, and hardly a word said, and no headstone. 'It's true, it always seemed to me to be . . . harsher than necessary. I would have paid for a headstone, at least for something to mark the place. To lie unmarked . . .'

'God knows the place.'

'I know He does. But men live among men. The social virtues are virtues.'

'Worldly concerns.'

'Yes, I know that's what you think. I believe our positions are quite well established.'

'Established, indeed. I know how you crave respectability. It is understandable, given what you've been, where you've been.'

'What I have been has no place here . . .' Matthew heard his own voice raised and stopped himself. It was so tiring talking to Oswald, who scoured Matthew's words for weakness, for the double meanings that betrayed his sin. He was now, as always, seeking some kind of victory that Matthew had learned he could withhold from him simply by remaining genial, cheerful, apparently

63

unconcerned. If he appeared not to be on the battlefield, how could he lose the battle? 'Perhaps some other topic over dinner,' he said, clapping his brother on the back.

*   *   *

The worldliness of Matthew and his family was confirmed in detail to Oswald when they were all gathered round the dinner table. Both of the elder daughters wore lace shawls, had lace handkerchiefs, and wore brooches. Even the stolid, sensible son (whom Matthew had described as industrious and dutiful and therefore—here he poured on the warm oil of flattery—resembling himself, Oswald) appeared to have ivory buttons adorning his waistcoat. Oswald did not know which suspicion he favoured, or which was worse: that his brother was successful enough to finance an extravagant home life or that he was again running up debts. Perhaps he would ask for money— Oswald rather expected that—and to that request could come only one answer. A man who has been imprisoned for debt, no matter how long ago, should have learned to live more circumspectly, more within his bounds.

Oswald declined a refilling of his wine glass by covering it with a swift hand. The movement was sharp and attracted attention. He thought that sufficient comment. Matthew suspected that he drank more freely in other company and saw rhetoric in his brother's stiff comportment. James, Dora's betrothed, did drink wine—Matthew Allen watched him doing so—drank it with the quiet commitment of a frightened, shy man, grasping the bottle whenever it was near. Really his lack of spirit was disappointing. He hoped Oswald wasn't watching too closely this dull new addition to the family. He decided to distract him by forcing him to compliment his wife.

'Most delicious,' he said.

'Yes, indeed,' Oswald chimed in on cue, but adulterated his praise. 'What is it precisely?'

'Boiled fowls,' she answered brightly. 'Nothing out of the ordinary. If I'd known you were coming, perhaps we could have produced more of a banquet.'

'Oh, no doubt, but really there is no need on my account.'

'Abigail, do sit up and chew properly.'

'So, Uncle Oswald,' Hannah began, deciding in her boredom to break the crust of tedious adult conversation, 'you must have many stories of Father when he was young.'

'Ah, well,' he dabbed at his mouth with his napkin, 'there is such a thing as discretion and familial loyalty.'

'I hadn't mean anything shameful.'

Oswald compressed his lips at that, embarrassed. 'No, I hadn't meant . . .'

'But if they are, I'm sure that would be even more interesting.'

'Well . . .'

A hot spurt in Matthew's chest: cringing in hiding, running, reprimands. What of that mess would Oswald drag out with his slow, relishing words? Perhaps the endless exclusions. Sandemanians required the congregation to be one in spirit, those who were not were required to leave. Matthew remembered the wooden meeting

65

house at the moor's edge, the blunted fervour of their voices inside as he wandered outside, exultant and ashamed. But that was the mess, perhaps, of every child's life. He knew that from his patients' unbosomings, and had heard much worse. It was Oswald's pretence that Oswald had never been a child.

'Hannah, really,' her mother chastised.

'Do we have to?' Matthew asked, his eyes quick around the table.

'Have no fear, younger brother, I shan't divulge your darkest secrets.'

'Oh, please do.' Hannah clapped her hands.

'No, no. Although there was one occasion . . . I recall that your father was always strong-willed and not, let us say, unspotted by the smaller sins.'

'Who among us could claim to be?' Matthew reasonably asked.

'He had a teacher when he was small . . .'

'Oh, I know what you're about to say,' Matthew interjected. 'The man was a savage. I left every class bruised.'

'And that being the case, it was natural that your father, being your father, would not leave his feelings unexpressed. Opportunity came when writing pattern letters.'

'What are pattern letters?' Abigail asked, holding her fork vertically on the table by her head like a tiny halberdier. Evidently she was listening with a keen degree of interest.

Oswald looked down at the infant seated there. A typically pointless and ill-disciplined defiance of convention to have at table with them a child who ought to be in the nursery.

'It's when you practise writing different kinds of

66

letters that you would send to different people,' Hannah explained.

'This was a letter to a magistrate,' Oswald resumed, 'so you can imagine what followed. The letter implored the full weight of the law to be laid upon Mr Mathers for his violent and disorderly conduct.'

Eliza laughed. 'I should think so. Beating poor Matthew.'

'It availed naught, though.' Matthew offered the postscript. 'I remember his conduct for some weeks after was far from improved.' He laughed along with the others, venting relief also that the anecdote hadn't been very much worse. He met his brother's gaze, which was warm but darkly eloquent with what had not been said. Even then Matthew found some recompense: he indicated with a finger where a pearl of fat hung from his brother's moustache.

*   *   *

The damp had soaked into Oswald's beard; it hung sparsely down, bedraggled plumage. Matthew ran a hand down the cold threads of his own beard, tugged it out at the chin.

'And what are the trees here?' Oswald asked with a vague encompassing wave.

'Well, that there,' Matthew replied, pointing with his stick at the thick dark cylinder of one, 'is a hornbeam.'

'Ah, yes.'

'Very hard wood. It's being used now for machine parts. There's a manufactury not too far from here.'

'Is there? Is there?'

They followed the wet path round, treading the rotted black leaves, back towards Fairmead House. Matthew Allen spied ahead of them two very acceptable patients for them to run into: the Tennyson brothers. But what were they doing with their faces? They walked with hesitant short steps as though half-blind, despite having their hands clasped against their cheeks, their eyes pulled open as far as possible between spread fingers.

'Good morning,' Allen called to them. They looked at him at first with those huge squirming eyes like sea monsters, then dropped their hands.

'What on earth . . .' Oswald muttered to himself.

Matthew strode forward to meet them. 'Do you mind if I enquire . . .' he began jovially.

Alfred explained, unembarrassed, as silent Septimus loitered behind his shoulder. 'It's something we used to do as boys. I'd just reminded Sep of it.'

'To help you see better?'

'Precisely.'

'And does it?'

'Good morning,' Alfred said to Oswald, who had arrived and stood, arms folded. 'It does mean that you can't not see. In so far as you ever can.'

'I see. Hunting that Grand Agent.' Allen smiled, although Alfred hung his head a little shyly at that. 'Gentlemen, allow me to introduce my brother, Mr Oswald Allen. Oswald, this is Alfred and Septimus Tennyson.'

'Very pleased to make your acquaintance, I'm sure.'

Alfred Tennyson raised his hand, compelling Oswald to unfold his arms and shake hands with the tall, peculiar brothers. Afterwards he clasped his hands behind his back and stood surveyingly, a visiting dignitary.

'And how are you feeling today, Septimus? You look in better spirits.'

Before Septimus could answer, a wood pigeon clattered out of the tree above their heads. Septimus cringed at the noise, then smiled. He made a gesture, softly raising his hands and floating them apart, half-apology, half-explanation. But Matthew waited him out, required that he should talk. Septimus looked again at the tattered leaves around his feet and said in a whisper, tangentially but positively, 'I like the winter.'

'Very good. Well, good day to you both. I shall leave you to your excursion.'

Walking on into the asylum grounds, Matthew explained to his brother whom they had just met, but not before Oswald had asked, 'What on earth were they doing with their faces?'

'They explained, didn't they? Or were you still catching up?' Matthew glanced at Oswald's worried face and felt, oddly, a flush of affection for him. Oswald was always frightened, scared and strict. Even as a little boy he was serious and orderly; alarmed by their father's ringing voice and fervour, he lived quietly within a set of reassuring rules of his own devising. Matthew pictured him as a child: combed head, woollen suit, the dark nervous gaze mutely requesting calm, peace, things done properly, and found the picture endearing.

'They're the Tennysons,' he went on. 'A Lincolnshire family. And quite a family. My word, the things I've been hearing from Septimus. Opium. Spirits. A menagerie also. A monkey.

Owls. Innumerable dogs. They're nobility somewhere along the line, in part degenerate. The brother Alfred is a poet, starting to elbow his way into the world. Great things are predicted by some, mostly his friends from Cambridge. It's a shame you won't be staying for longer. There's a literary evening I frequent in Bedford Square.'

Oswald had not particularly listened, hearing only the little missiles of 'nobility', 'Cambridge', 'Bedford Square'.

'Yes, yes. Well, there we are.'

'I'm sorry?'

'I'm very pleased for you that you are acquainted with the minor nobility. You must be very proud.'

'Oswald, really. Septimus is a patient.'

'Of course. Of course.' Oswald stopped, looked up into his brother's face. 'Another opportunity for your dreadful pride. Another chance for you to humiliate me.'

'Oswald, what on earth are you talking about?'

'Don't play that game with me, Matthew.' Oswald was shouting now, his face white and spiteful. 'You may have established yourself in this respectable situation, the good doctor, but don't forget that I know who you are. No doubt you have contracted sizeable debts to create all this. Just know that you won't get a penny out of me.'

Oswald was as boring as the mad, with one thought choking him, controlling him, blaring out of him. Matthew tried to remain dispassionate, tried to chuckle even, but it was difficult. His brother's face was so familiar, so powerful, and his words once again loosened his past into this place, and Matthew was so tired of the mad.

'Yes. Don't forget that I know who you are.

70

Literary evenings in Bedford Square! Matthew Allen. I'm sure your new friends would be intrigued by the history of your debts, your imprisonments.'

That was too much. Matthew grabbed at his brother's lapels. Oswald skidded back on the wet path, but Matthew held him upright, his fingertips bending painfully under the thick cloth. 'Just you . . . just you . . .' Matthew's vision of the moment was strangely glazed. There, at the end of his arms, was his brother's face, so familiar but thickened with age, he saw. He heard his own breathing, the soft crackling of twigs underfoot. He heard his son Fulton saying, 'Father.' Matthew dropped Oswald quickly back onto the flats of his feet. Fulton approached. As he did so, Oswald, as in victory, smiled.

'Father, you're wanted back at the house.'

*   *   *

Matthew Allen lay and felt his weight entirely sustained, his head sunk in the pillow, his four limbs dead still, washed up there like driftwood. Bed was always a pleasure, an island he reached after the variable inevitable storms of a day spent with the mad, their frantic, tunnelling logic, their sorrow, their hopelessness and aggression and indecencies. No muscles had to work to keep him there. The lamps hissed quietly. Beside him on the pillow was the familiar peaceful landscape of Eliza's face: soft, straight eyebrows, fine nostrils, the neat volute that ran down from them to the large, warm, mobile mouth. With her hair pinned, her nightcap on, her face at bedtime was presented

71

with a kind of ceremonial or surgical simplicity that could strike him as funny. It was the cap particularly that made her look cute, childish or comically ecclesiastical. Her haughty, lordly, stern expression when asleep could also amuse him.

'What are you peering at?' she asked.

'Only you. Can't a man peer at his wife?'

'Why? Do I look . . . is there something?'

'No, no. You look very nice.'

'Oh well, then. He'll be gone tomorrow morning.'

'Yes, he will.'

'And he hasn't been so terrible.'

'Oh, yes, he has. I can't wait to pack him off. Spiteful, resentful man.'

'Really?'

'You don't know the half of it.'

'So what is there to tell me?'

'Nothing. There's nothing to tell you, nothing that needs to be told.'

'Well, I'm sorry he's been horrid.'

'Not that he can help it.'

'Poor battered old cat,' she said. She petted his head, lay softly against his side.

'Mm. That's nice.'

'Yes,' she said pouting.

Matthew reached a hand down and laid it on the warm width of her thigh. The flesh was so smooth under the sliding soft fabric. 'Very soothing.'

*   *   *

Oswald Allen's farewell was surprisingly gracious. He handed out sixpences to the children, even though only Abigail was young enough to be delighted. He thanked Eliza for the hospitality of her home and invited them all to visit in York.

Matthew and Eliza walked him to the station—again he insisted that they should not get a carriage for him—and during that walk the silences did lengthen uncomfortably. But Oswald could act as though absorbed in details of the scene, the motionless cold cattle, the ponds and their withered reeds, the passers-by.

Seated in his carriage, he raised a gloved hand to wave. The glove was buttoned at the side, his coat buttoned at the front, his collar firm beneath his chin. Matthew felt he had him strait-jacketed and safely stowed for transportation. In profile, Oswald opened a small volume, presumably devotional, and began to read.

'Yes, yes,' said Matthew to himself. 'Off you go.'

The train hissed, clanked, and its four carriages rumbled away towards London. The platform filled with steam. Like a genie in a cloud, Oswald was gone.

'I don't expect we will see him again for some time.'

'You're forgetting the wedding.'

'So I am.' The wedding. For which he needed money.

*   *   *

Nobody wanted to play. Abigail's attentions slid off her father. She clambered up his legs, received a quick flinch of a smile, and was handed down again. Even her trick of folding his ear so that the top bendy part touched the bottom bendy part only resulted in a stubborn horse's shake of the head and a reprimand for disturbing his papers, which she hadn't done in her opinion. He apologised when she told him, even smiled at her, and pressed a firm, furry kiss to her forehead, but after that he sent her away.

Hannah wasn't anywhere to be found and her mother was little better, talking tediously with Dora. Abigail pulled at her mother's skirts and was firmly disengaged. Her mother then fetched her outdoor clothes, fitted her into them, deafening Abigail as she fastened her hat, and ushered her out to run around in the gardens.

Snow. Fresh snow that covered the gaps in the old snow and shone evenly everywhere. Abigail squinted at the hard bounce of bright light, breathed the sparkling, almost painful air. She ran a little way to stamp her footprints, looked back at them, continued onto the lawn, which gave way differently under her so that she stumbled, whitening her knees and mittens. She tasted the snow on her palms: a nothing taste, but full of an unnameable big thing, full of distance, full of the sky. Quickly it soaked through the wool and chilled her skin. She rubbed her hands on her coat and set off running again—she'd remembered the water pump by Fairmead House.

Yes, there were! There were icicles hanging from its nose. They were smooth at the top and tapered down, with bulges, like a pea pod, to a stopped drop round as a glass bead. She snapped one off and sucked it, holding it along her tongue until she could drink its melt.

The idiot Simon found her there. He looked padded and enormous in his coat, gloves and hat pulled down tight. Abigail showed him the icicles and he snapped one off as well. It darted out of his grasp and he had to pick it up from the snow to eat it. 'Cold,' he said.

'Shall we make a snowman?' Abigail asked.

Simon shook his head.

'Oh, please. Oh, please.'

Simon shook his head again. 'Do a cat,' he said.

So together they rolled two balls that peeled up the snow from the ground, one big and one small. Simon set the small one on top of the larger. With soaked hands that itched and tingled and that she shook when they were too cold, Abigail helped to make the triangular ears to put on top. But then Simon wouldn't let her do any more; he had to be in charge of everything. He tried to put the last three icicles in for whiskers, but that was uneven and anyway they stuck straight out and, after pauses, dropped off. Abigail didn't think it looked much like a cat in the end, more like a snowman with silly ears.

*   *   *

When Matthew Allen had the idea he stood up out of his chair. Was it workable? Of course it was workable. Hadn't he read of similar? All the elements of it were there, scattered through journals and treatises and out in the world, before his very eyes, hidden in plain sight. All of a sudden they had flown together in his mind, bolted together in this singular, hotly alloyed, all-solving thought. His body clenched with excitement, as though gripping the thought inside him so as not to lose it. Then he applauded the ramifications, the social aspect, the spiritual, the financial, the end to boredom, actually clapped his hands. Yes, indeed.

He couldn't possibly keep still, so skipped off for a walk. Without hat or coat he left his study and stepped out into the white morning.

The world was sharply displayed. Frost on the lawn, each and every blade of grass, each single one of them crusted with crystals. It creaked underfoot, fracturing. He pressed down, crushed and dissolved the ice with each step and left behind footprints—he looked back at them—of mineral green, of wet malachite. He rubbed his hands and laughed as he walked. There they were, the trees, beautiful friends, out there all this time, waiting to receive him. Ranks of lean footmen, they awaited his instructions. Their leafless twigs bounced responsively in the wind in front of a scratched, white sky. In one of them small birds, titmice, swapped their places, switching back and forth, then flew off together in a pretty wave of panic. His eye followed them and saw a hunched, short figure walking towards him from Fairmead House. He knew that gait, the weight carried low around the hips, the strides balanced and forthright, the shoulders held tensely up to carry the burdensome head. John Clare.

John approached the doctor who looked remarkably animated, without overcoat or hat, dancing on the spot to keep warm, blowing warmth over his hands and intermittently smiling. Perhaps he had the good news he'd been yearning for, despising himself for wanting it, but unable to prevent the painful increase of hope.

'Good morning, doctor.'

'Yes, indeed. It is, it is. Beautiful morning.' He inhaled theatrically through quivering arched nostrils. The air entered his head and chest in delightful lengths of chilly clarity. He felt very tall and awake.

'Do you have something for me?'

'I'm sorry?'

'I mean, has anything come for me from, you know . . . ?'

'Oh, yes. Oh, yes, I actually do. A letter arrived for you yesterday, but I didn't see you. Here it is.' Allen reached into his jacket pocket. 'I don't know who it's from.'

John took the letter. No sender's address on the back. 'Are you not cold?' he asked when he looked up again. The doctor had his hands tucked into his armpits, was jiggling his legs.

'Yes, I suppose I am. Shall we go inside, have some tea, perhaps?'

Inside, Dr Allen led the way to the kitchen, John trundling after in his wake. Allen shooed the cook and her girls out of the way and set about making tea himself, humming as he popped open the caddy, unhooked cups from the shelf. John sat down at the table, clasped his hands with the letter between them, and looked towards the girls huddled against one wall, talking from the corners of their mouths. He wanted to make some sign of his being one of them. By his posture he tried to demonstrate this, holding himself tightly in place, an awkwardly wrapped parcel of a man carried in and left there. But they wouldn't meet his gaze. No, they could barely see him. This wasn't how it used to be: the times he'd been embarrassed by the clumping of his hob-nailed boots on the polished floors of his noble patrons, an unlikely prodigy invited across the divide for conversation and inspection, then delivered to the servants' quarters to be fed before he walked back to his cottage. Then, he'd felt the muscles of his face, stiff from smiling, relax as he chewed bread and bacon, allowed to forget himself as he listened to their conversation. But he wasn't a country man any more, or even a poet. What they saw, if they saw him at all, was one of the doctor's patients, a madman.

Ignoring them now, he opened the letter.

Most esteemed poet, Mr John Clare,
Like you I am a simple man, outwardly at least. I hope that you will forgive my great temerity in addressing you. Be assured I do not take up my pen without trepidation!
I am a labouring man of the county of Dorset. I make my living as a farmhand as you yourself did if I'm not much mistaken, but this is not the end of my story. For many years I have had a strong predilection for the heavenly art of poetry and have worshipped at the Muses' temple. Some have been kind enough to say that my own efforts are not without merit, even genius . . .

Nothing. No help, no response from the literary world that had turned its back on him, cast him off to die in the wilderness. John skimmed down to the familiar request for assistance, and would he be good enough to cast his 'terrible eye' over the enclosed efforts? Might one of his friends, sympathetic to rural versing, be interested in publishing one of them?

'Tea,' Dr Allen said, handing John a cup.

John crumpled the letter into his pocket—later

78

he'd watch it blacken and curl on a fire—while the doctor remained standing, drinking quickly.

'Is there any news, perhaps?' John asked. 'Of those poems of mine that you'd sent to friends of yours?'

'Oh. Ah, yes. Yes, I'm sorry. It had quite slipped my mind.' John watched the doctor wrestle that persistent smile from his lips and knew that the answer would not be good. 'Yes, I'm afraid it seems that you were correct in your supposition that your type of genius is no longer the fashion. That fashion should have anything to do with such matters, of course, can only be deprecated in the strongest terms, but there are phases, I suppose . . .'

The doctor's high spirits now flowed into a disquisition on recent trends in literary taste while John, whose cup of tea was now an unwanted encumbrance, began composing loudly in his mind a reply to E. Higgins Esq. that would tell him precisely what he should know.

> . . . under no circumstances entrust the least of hopes . . . changeable whims . . . estrange you from your fellows . . . took from me my peace of mind, my native country, my wives . . .

*   *   *

It was still dark when Margaret awoke. She lay still for a moment, eyes open and dry, holding the upper edge of the bed clothes, discerning before she moved the soft grey outlines of her room.

The world is a room full of heavy furniture. Eventually you are allowed to leave.

She felt her own Silent Watcher lying there inside

79

her. That was what she called it, the thing that watched it all happen, that wanted her to live and sometimes let that be known, but could do nothing about it. It observed only, from deep behind her eyes. It had watched her husband's wet eyes as they bore down on her and had watched that time he made her eat rotten meat, already blue and green and stinking, iridescent with decay. It had watched and remembered that, and watched when he locked her in the outhouse. And watched when she took to spending days in the parish church and liked the calm safety in there.

She raised herself out of bed and released a quiet flow into her chamber pot. She walked over to her basin of water and broke its frail covering of ice. She undid the strings at her neck and lifted off her nightgown. She stood then naked and unable to see herself in the gloom, her body a shadow that held her from the floor. She picked up cold water and dropped it over her head and neck. It fell on her like blades. She loved the winter, the purity of its punishment, and the purity of being awake before the rest, a single candle burning. Her husband had been always there, doubling her, filling the lucid emptiness, and he could never stand the cold, swearing and stamping, whacking the fire to a blaze with the poker, drinking, eating, laughing with his red mouth, and hot as a wasp's tail at night, alone, stinging, stinging.

She patted herself dry. Her skin was smooth and numb. She put her nightdress on again. Holding the table edge, she lowered herself onto her knees to pray. The small wooden cross was a certain black form against the grey bloom of the wall. She fixed her eyes on it. She began.

80

*   *   *

Matthew Allen lifted his head and looked out at the morning. Beyond the blue lawn the trees were there. Their fine twigs, at this distance, made a russet mist. He looked back down at his page of calculations.

They added up to something, and that was with a very modest number of predicted orders. He smiled. He looked up again and saw a fox trotting silently across the lawn, its low body slung from its spine, its narrow head angled to the ground. How light it was in its movements, and quick, all travel and purpose.

*   *   *

John woke in a rage, knowing exactly where he was. He rolled out of bed, thumping his bare feet on the floorboards. He relieved himself into his chamber pot, clearing his throat and spitting also through the froth. He shunted it back under the bed with his toe against the warm china.

He rubbed his face in cold water from the jug, rubbed away at the dream still smeared across his thoughts. A girl with dark, unruly hair. She had secrets to tell him that he would understand. Her eyes glittered. His penis had stiffened as she brought her moist lips to his ear and whispered, words he could not now remember detonating softly inside his mind, urgent, full of meaning. Something to do with a place she could show him if he would just follow her. He'd wanted so much to know what she was saying that he'd woken up,

81

tense, tumescent, straining to follow. He opened his eyes now so as not to see the intimate dark shine of her eyes and feel her hair minutely touching him. He wetted down his own hair, then quickly dressed. Fully clothed, he sat back down on his bed. What could he do now? Where could he go? Just out. That would be enough. He had a key after all. He could wait in his room until after breakfast, cadge some bread from the kitchen girls, and head out and away.

*   *   *

William Stockdale finished polishing his boots by stretching a rag over the toe, holding the rag at both ends, and working it back and forth with a rapid milking action. Then the other foot. He tightened the trouser straps that hooked under his shoes between heel and sole.

He refolded the rag and placed it back in the drawer.

He swung his arms around, pivoting his body left-right, right-left at the hips. He windmilled his arms over and over to fill them with blood, his hands feeling heavier, more useful, once he had finished.

He neatened his jacket, tugged at his sleeves. Unlike the inmates, he wore his clothes with precision, correctly fastened and at the proper angles to his body.

He picked up his heavy ring of keys and went out. He locked his door behind him.

*   *   *

Hannah sat in front of her mirror and brushed her

hair. It hung in two drapes either side of a neat parting of white scalp that she thought too wide because of her hair's regrettable fineness. She brushed down from the top, fifty times on each side, until it was glossy and fluent, and, floating, followed her brush up as she lifted it away. When she was done the light set around it an even garland of shine.

With adept quick fingers she divided it again and wove two plaits with their roots at her temples. She left them hanging there while she swept the rest back over her ears and pinned it, then rolled the length that hung down her back into a rope and pinned it to her crown. Then she looped the two plaits under her ears, pinning them behind so that her ears were framed: delicate, white, sculptural.

She regarded herself, wearing the careful expression she maintained before mirrors—her lips pressed together and lowered, her eyes looking appealingly upwards, her face devoid of movement. She turned this frozen face from side to side and looked. Good enough. Unlikely to be better. Today she would make something happen. The situation was clear: there he was; here she was. It simply needed to begin.

*   *   *

John heard the gate swing shut, its lock grinding round again, and swift footsteps behind him. He moved from the path and hid behind a wide, wet trunk. Chewing on the hunk of bread that he struggled to moisten with sufficient saliva to swallow, he saw the right-angled figure of William Stockdale set off on his way, presumably, to the mythically worse place, Leopard's Hill Lodge. John leaned. A damp twig cracked softly under his boot. William Stockdale stopped. John ducked his head and pressed himself against the cold slime of the tree trunk. Again a fragment of the same twig split under his weight. He heard William Stockdale walk back the way he'd gone. He must have caught sight of John because there were a few quicker paces that scuffed through the leaves, then a thump on John's shoulder. He was pulled from behind the tree, almost lifted like a cat by its loose collar of skin as Stockdale wrenched with a strong grip on John's coat.

'I have a key,' John said. 'I have a key.'

'Then why are you hiding, you fool?'

'Look. Look.' John pulled the key from his pocket, dangled it in front of Stockdale on its frayed string.

'So why are you hiding?' William Stockdale let him go and brushed at his own jacket.

'I don't know.'

'I thought you were someone trying to make an escape.'

'No, I'm not.'

'Well, then. Just playing the fool.' He patted him harshly on the cheek.

Stockdale strode away again and John bent down to pick up his bread, brushing crumbs of broken leaf and earth from it and biting. He panted and cursed, struggling to swallow.

For hours as he walked, he re-enacted the incident with much more satisfying and violent conclusions. He could have unleashed his strength. He could have given Stockdale a lick of boxer John, and that would have shown him. Repeatedly

84

Stockdale staggered away, apologetic and impressed, feeling his face, blinking at the blood on his fingertips. John was magnanimous, feeling that as long as the blackguard had learned his lesson, they would say no more about it. Or he didn't, and John carried on until the man lay knocked out on the ground, breathing through scarlet bubbles.

*   *   *

Alfred swirled the branches around him. His cape caught up behind him in the wind imparted the sensation almost of having wings. He pressed his steps down to the sides and his skates bore him over the ice with a fine sound of grinding stone. It broke up the thickness of his blood to move like this, to feel the sharp winterness of the day. Scribbling to himself, turning his patterns over his frozen pond, he could almost not think of Arthur, his dear, dead friend Arthur Hallam, who would not leave his thoughts.

As his revolve carried him round to the far side of the pond he was startled by a girl's shape dark against the tarnished silver of the sky. He slowed towards her. She stood quite still, above him on the bank. 'Good afternoon?' he asked.

His dark eyes, wind-polished, shone in the clayish yellow of his face. 'Good afternoon,' Hannah said.

'Yes?'

'I've come . . .'

'You're Allen's daughter, aren't you, the fair What-was-it?'

'. . . to pay you a visit. I've come to pay you a visit.

85

In case . . .'

'I see. Do you have a message?'

'No. In case you are lonely.'

'I see. You've come to pay me a visit.'

'That's right.'

'And it is . . . ?'

'Hannah.'

'Hannah. Of course it is.'

Curious, he leaned forward precariously to get her face into focus. He saw her pale lips fluttering as she drew in a breath and backed ever so slightly away. 'You're cold,' he said. 'Shall we go in?'

She nodded.

'One moment.' He skated away to an easier point of exit. She walked around to meet him and silently offered a hand to help him out, but he didn't see it and hobbled up onto the grass unaided. Together they walked back to the house, Tennyson teetering over the girl, who wondered why he didn't think to unstrap his skates and walk comfortably in his boots, but said nothing. She walked beside him proudly at his careful slow pace, as though in a procession, and was only slightly distracted by the sweet-sharp human odour that came from his clothes. At the door he finally did remove his skates, bending down so that she could see the top of his head. Thick hair, actually thick hairs—a wide diameter to each hair—flowed from the crown in strong waves. A leaf fragment had somehow lodged in there. She wanted to tease it out with her fingers, but of course could not, nor could she say anything.

Tennyson opened the door and ushered her in. She entered looking hungrily at everything for signs of the remarkable life that was lived there, but found an ordinary vestibule—wallpaper, a table, a mirror. There on the antlers of the coatstand, however, hung his coats and that wide black hat. He twirled the cape from his shoulders and added it. With proper care, with gentle fingers that seemed unafraid as he touched her shoulders, he took her coat from her and draped it beside his own. 'Thank you,' she whispered.

His gentlemanly etiquette appeared variable: he now led the way, striding ahead rather than walking behind her quietly directing, and she had to hurry after. She was rewarded, though, when she followed him into a room that was most certainly inhabited by a poet. As he bent to the fire, positioning fresh logs with his hands so that afterwards he had to wipe smuts and blown ash from them onto his trouser fronts, she looked around at a gracious, intellectual disorder. The piles of books and papers, the rumpled sofa and littered desk, the short-stemmed pipes that roosted on nests of ash and spent spills on ledges all around the room, showed this to be a working room, its objects gathered without thought of their effect. The room absolutely radiated from him, now stalking about its centre, thumping cushions. It flowed from him, and visiting it without him there would have been like listening into his thoughts or hearing about him from his friends. And on the desk, in that big open ledger that looked like a butcher's book—could that be a new poem? Certainly the lines did not cross to the far side of the page. His handwriting. The charged page vibrated in her sight. A poem lived on it. If she could walk across and read those fresh words, seen by no one besides herself and the poet who chose them, they would sing through her mind. What sentiments might they express?

'Do take a seat,' he said, 'and I'll arrange some tea.'

Having pulled the servants' bell, he sat down on the sofa opposite the seat on which she'd perched. He stretched his long legs in front of him, crossed at the ankles, and pushed his fingers through his hair, passing tantalisingly beside but not finding the bit of vegetation she'd seen at the door.

'So, you're Dr Allen's daughter,' he repeated.

'Yes, I am.'

The door opened. A servant entered, a woman. An old woman, white-haired, raw-handed, ruddy streaks in her face from the cold day and the kitchen fire, she looked at them quickly and curtsied.

'Ah, Mrs Yates.'

Mrs Yates nodded her head slowly, looking across at her master and his young female guest. Hannah, shamed, stared down at her knees, plucked her skirt straight with brisk, matter-of-fact fingers, attempting an unconcerned composure. She hadn't thought of them being seen by anyone.

'Yes, as you see, we are entertaining this afternoon. So tea, please, and et cetera. Plenty of et cetera, if you'd be so good. Skating has sharpened the appetite.'

'Very good, sir.'

Mrs Yates backed out of the room. Tennyson smiled at Hannah. He looked as if he were about to say something. Hannah sat with her head very erect, her neck stretched as long, as much like Annabella's as possible, and waited. But Tennyson didn't say anything. Instead, his gaze wandered to

88

the fire. Fortunately Hannah had prepared some questions.

'How are you finding the area, Mr Tennyson?'

'Oh, very well.' He looked back at her. 'Pleasant enough.'

She blushed. 'Have you visited Copt Hall?' she asked.

'No, I can't say that I have.'

'I understand it is where *A Midsummer Night's Dream* was first performed, for a wedding. It is a beautiful house in the forest. You can walk quite easily . . .'

He woke up at that, leaned forward with widened eyes. She felt that stare inside her; it buzzed against her spine. 'So they were all here, were they? Hermia and Lysander and the others were all lost in these woods. Puck appearing on a branch. Oh, I am pleased you told me that.'

*   *   *

Her stomach empty, her body light and thin, Margaret stood in the forest and looked up at bare, spreading branches and thought of Christ's body hanging there, hanging from its five wounds. The thorns, like those thorns over there, wound round Him in a tight crown must have infested His head with pain. And the wounds of the nails, driven into His poor, innocent body by the hammering of Sin. They held Him up. He hung from them. This thought enlarged suddenly—they were *how* He hung in the world: it was His wounds, His pain, that connected Him to the world. She felt this in herself, that at her points of contact with the world she was in pain, that her soul was pinned to the wall of her flesh, suffering, suffocating for release. She knotted her fingers tightly together, swaying in the strength of this thought. She breathed hissingly through her teeth, grateful for this illumination, and wanting more.

*　　　*　　　*

Abigail sat on the rug by the fire playing with her dolls and half-listening to her parents' talk. The heat from the fire reddened her left cheek, made the skin feel tight, her clothes dry and crisp. If she didn't move, it made a white light shine in a corner of her head. She knew that sitting there made the rest of the room seem dark and cold like cold water, and she liked that. Her dolls' bead eyes gleamed in the firelight as she bowed them towards each other and made them talk. 'No, don't say that, Angelica . . .'

'One consequence of course might very well be the renewal of my lecturing,' Matthew said.

'Might be,' Eliza stroked the top of her husband's head as she passed, then sat down beside him, 'if it all succeeds in the way you imagine.'

'If!' he repeated. 'If!' Eliza could be cold towards his enthusiasms until he was proved correct.

'Well,' she said slowly, teasing, 'one never can tell.'

'Oh, yes, one can. Primo, there are several other companies out there already operating, which tells us that it is viable. Secundo, I have advantages over their schemes, which means that I will supersede them before very long. So don't you doubt this for one instant, and be assured,' he went on, wagging a finger, 'that my services as a speaker will be required around the country.'

'What scheme?' Fulton asked, entering with a book in hand.

'Ah, yes, my son. All shall be revealed. It may very well come to constitute a significant part of your future and fortune.'

'Why not tell me now? Why keep me in ignorance?' Fulton balled his fists quietly in his pockets.

'No, no. A little more secrecy, a chrysalis for this larva. I'll just say this . . . it is a kind of a machine.'

'An engine? A machine?'

Abigail, now listening, added this to her dialogue. 'A machine to make cakes,' she said. 'But shh, it's a secret.'

'Abigail, don't sit so close to the fire. You'll burn to ashes,' Eliza said, and turned back.

Abigail looked up in terror, and shuffled quickly forward on her behind.

'Not really burn,' Eliza reassured her.

'It was a figure of speech,' her father explained.

The adults smiled fondly, Fulton included, who now felt half-appeased and part of their conspiracy, whatever it was.

*　　　*　　　*

The two horses stood nose to rump beside each other with blankets over their backs, a little ice in their coarse eyelashes. They blinked with effort over their downcast, convex eyes as John passed, patting them, and headed on to the silent camp.

Men sat around the yellow fire, leaning forwards,

91

staring into it, thick blankets across their backs also.

'Ezekiel?' John asked.

'You've found me,' said one figure, turning. 'Ah, John Clare. You've come among us again.'

'I have.'

'There's little food now, I'm afraid to tell you. Are you come hungry?'

John attempted to say no, but a moment's hesitation gave him away.

'Ah, you are. We've a little meat. I'll put the pan on. We'll be bringing more later, sweet little hotchiwitchis. Time of year for them. But to keep your soul in your body till then.'

Ezekiel reached for a greasy black frying pan and knocked it down on the fire until it lay flat on the burning wood. John sat down on a log beside another man, smiling generally to show his friendliness. He held his white hands out towards the snapping flames. Ezekiel rose to his feet. Keeping his blanket around him, he ambled off to a varda and returned with a piece of venison now putrid and stinking. He pulled a knife from his pocket and shaved fine strips of the discoloured meat and tossed them into the pan where they hissed and curled. When they were cooked black, John was invited to pluck them out with his fingers and eat. They tasted only of the charring, were quite palatable and hot. John ate them and sucked his fingers.

'Cold enough to wither you,' Ezekiel said.

John wiped his mouth with the back of his hand. 'We should fight,' he said, still bellicose from his encounter with Stockdale earlier. 'Spar a bit,' he went on. 'Are there no prize-fighting men among you?' He stood up and feinted a few blows with half-closed fists. 'Come on, one of you. Let's see a bit of pluck.'

The men laughed. 'One of our crew is in that sport,' Ezekiel said. 'Travels the fairs. Makes money with his iron head.'

'No sense to knock out of it,' added one of the others.

'Jeremiah,' another man explained. 'Fights as the Gypsy Baron.'

'I'll see how quick your hands are, John Clare,' said Ezekiel standing, hunching his shoulder up under his ears and raising two stiff fists far in front of his body.

'Good lad,' John said, curving right hooks through the mist of his breath.

*   *   *

'That smells powerful,' Hannah said, smiling through thin, smarted tears. 'Do you smoke a particular type of tobacco?'

'Important thing is,' Tennyson replied, lifting his pipe from his lower lip, 'to dry it out for a while beforehand. Then you get a good full flavour.'

'I see.'

With the tea things cleared away, Tennyson smoking, and the dim early evening light falling heavily into that untidy room, the conversation was now hard to keep alive. Hannah felt isolated on her chair. He produced smoke in incredible volume and it was the strongest Hannah had ever smelled. It scraped her throat while he sat calmly at its source, far away, silent, his gaze unfocused. She had lost him to the marine element of his

93

private thought. And the silence was thickening, becoming harder and harder to break. In her imagining beforehand the conversation was supposed to have become music by this point, a duet, but their voices now were separate and sparse. She thought of a question that might startle him into a renewed appreciation of her. He would know at least how advanced, how daring she was.

'May I ask you, what is your opinion of Lord Byron's poetry?'

He did indeed raise both eyebrows at that, blowing long cones of smoke from his nostrils. He answered quite wonderfully with a revelation.

'A very great deal. His poetry, well . . .' Here he perhaps decided against a critical disquisition. She thought he might not think her up to it, but what he said instead pleased her just as well. 'I remember when he died. I was a lad. I walked out into the woods full of distress at the news. It was the thought of all he hadn't yet written, all bright inside him, being lost for ever, lowered into darkness for eternity. I was most gloomy and despondent. I scratched his name onto a rock, a sandstone rock. It must still be there, I should think.'

*   *   *

Ezekiel returned with two panting terriers and a sack over his shoulder. The dogs leaned against his ankles as he dumped the contents onto the ground. Three hedgehogs bounced heavily. Ezekiel picked one up with his coat sleeve pulled down over his hand.

'Told you,' he said. 'Best time of year for them.

Good thick fat on him, get through the winter. Here, let them settle a moment.'

He put it down with the other two and waited, whispering, 'Come on, old boys, don't be feared' to them while the prickly balls loosened, long reaching feet were planted on the ground, and shy, snuffling faces emerged. With a thick short stick he knocked the head of one. Then with a knife he cut around the back of its neck, pushed downwards through its spine, turned it and split along its belly. He pocketed his knife and pulled the head down, removing spine and guts together, and tossed aside the expressionless face and dangling violet tubes. The dogs chased the scrap. The body he gave to Judith to pack in stiff clay and went on to the next one. Judith made a smooth ball around the animal and placed it in the fire.

'Good for clay round here. Good sticky yellow stuff.'

'Northamptonshire gypsies,' John said, 'bury the balls under the fire in a little pit.'

'Do they now. They have their ways, I suppose, but they're wasting time. Come out perfect like this.'

An hour later the baked spheres were rolled out of the fire with a stick, cracked open, and the cooked hedgehogs were lifted out naked and steaming. Their prickles remained stuck in the clay and pulled easily from the flesh. Judith made slices through their stippled backs and the fine-smelling meat was passed around.

John ate. It tasted as well as he'd remembered: a sweet, earthen, secret flavour. The meat was tender. Warm grease coated his lips.

'Told you him had good pork on him,' Ezekiel

said, eating a slice from the side of his knife.

A bottle of whisky was passed around to accompany the food. John took a swig, letting its fire wash loosely down into his chest. 'Old John Barleycorn,' he said, saluting with the bottle. 'Now there's a fighting man. Seen him dust out many a strong fellow.' The others laughed.

'Let's be having you, then,' he said, standing, raising his fists.

'Oho. Someone's keen,' Ezekiel answered. 'Anybody want to take him on?'

'Come on,' John implored. There was anger inside him. He wanted to hit. 'Someone here must have some bottom.' He dabbed the air in front of him with soft feints, quick combinations.

'I'll give you some exercise, my friend,' one man answered, rising.

'Good man, Tom. John, this is Thomas Lee.'

John shook hands with his opponent and backed away. The man was large, handsome, smiling loosely, with a dark fleece of hair. Might be he was slow. Around them the gypsies started to whistle and cheer. John's blood raced now. He tilted his head, focusing. The stone-cold air scraped his lungs. Thomas Lee paced slow from side to side, shrugging with his fists around his hips. He stepped forward, threw out a blow. John ducked it, stepped in, landed a punch full force on the buttons of Thomas Lee's coat. Thomas Lee grinned, pushing John back by his shoulders. Then he loosed a punch into him that whacked John's sternum, making him step back further. The stout contact pleased John, who stepped forward again, bobbing behind his fists, watched, planted his feet, swayed from his hips, watched, and darted in again, swinging. His left fist caught the cold stubbled bone of Tom's jaw. And then the fight began, both men neglecting their guards as they flurried forth punches. When John couldn't avoid Tom's, which mostly he couldn't, he leaned forward fractionally, affectionately into the blows. That way, after a minute or two branches flailed upwards and the hard wet ground thumped along John's back. He stood up laughing, to applause, his head ringing, the sweet taste of blood on his lips. Again he went at Tom. Again a well-landed fist tilted everything up and beneath him.

Ezekiel gripped his shoulder. 'Come and have a swallow, little John.'

John panted, looked across. Tom was also walking back. 'Very well. Very well, Robin.'

'Hey?'

'Little John. Robin of Sherwood.'

Ezekiel helped John up like an old dame, lifting him by his upper arm.

Back beside the fire, John looked around at the faces flaring with the flames, each so distinctive. How they emerged from the night's darkness, gathered there in their makeshift camp. Tom patted him heavily on the shoulder and sat. They sang. A child raised John's arm as champion. Again there was cheering and laughter. John swilled whisky, spat blood, swilled again and swallowed.

Later John stretched out under thick blankets, his mind marked with the blotchy images, leaching at their edges, and parroting, repetitious phrases— *have you the pluck? have you the pluck?*—of exhausted thought.

Tennyson sat and smoked on in the darkening room after the girl had left. The logs in the fireplace shifted with a rustling collapse. His large left hand lay on his knee; his right held the warm bowl of his pipe.

It had been an odd visitation. Certainly it had broken up his solitude and hadn't been unwelcome. Perhaps she was lonely also, or bored. She'd been very eager to discuss poetry. Maybe she lacked for such conversation. Too much of that, though, and she'd turn bluestocking, fit only for a literary man and what sort of a life was that? Curious girl. Very pale skin. Whitely her narrow face had glowed in the gloom. He thought of her living out here in the woods, surrounded by the mad. An interesting subject. He pictured her again, this time in white, her hair a red rope down her back, glimmering through the woodland shade—not that 'woodland shade' would do at all. Barred from the world by the cagework of trees, by ancient trees, the sunset obscured by their limbs. The forest. The silent paths. The mad. Where minds decay and leaves rot. Fat weeds rotting at Lethe's wharf.

The figment's loneliness merged with his own; lyrical, it wandered in the room, wreathed in his smoke. He thought about her and words for her for a while, then picked up his notebook. He leafed through it a moment and found the first poem he'd written after his friend Arthur's death, about his body returning from Trieste. He punched his thigh. There it was, complete and finished and shut. He wanted that feeling again, of bringing Arthur close in words, and of making something whole out of the drag and drift, the shapeless spill of his life. He wanted Arthur. The poem was, what, six years old now, seven? He felt the strength go out of him.

Fair ship that from the Italian shore
  Sailest the placid ocean-plains
  With my lost Arthur's loved remains,
Spread thy full wings, and waft him o'er.

So draw him home to those that mourn
  In vain; a favourable speed
  Ruffle thy mirror'd mast, and lead
Thro' prosperous floods his holy urn.

All night no ruder air perplex
  Thy sliding keel, till Phosphor, bright
  As our pure love, thro' early light
Shall glimmer on the dewy decks.

Sphere all you lights around, above;
  Sleep, gentle heavens, before the prow;
  Sleep, gentle winds, as he sleeps now,
My friend, the brother of my love;

My Arthur, whom I shall not see
  Till all my widow'd race be run;
  Dear as the mother to the son,
More than my brothers are to me.

*   *   *

John stood in a gold cloud of his own breath. Dawn. A heavy low sun seemingly at head-height. He couldn't see clearly. His left eye looked

99

through a knife slit, his vision narrowed between a pinkish mist. One side of his body was numb. The cold air was flowing into his mouth, making his teeth tingle. He felt with his fingers: his lip was swollen up into a sneer that exposed his bite. And where was he? Some sort of encampment. He wondered how he'd got there. It had something to do, didn't it, with his being a prize fighter. Had he fought a bout there? That looked like the ashes of a night's fire under the new-fallen snow. There were caravans and horses. Gypsies must have put on the bout. He checked his knuckles for grazes and swelling. They looked good. The trees swung their billy clubs all the right the wind shoved have you the pluck Old Jack Randall will Jack Randall must have the pluck to come up to the scratch most famous fighter of them all must have dusted them out pretty quick! Old Jack Randall would have wouldn't he what with the strength in his arms no question he stood up straight Jack Randall. He bounced up and down, threw out a few punches, though his head ached. He was ready to go again with whoever would challenge him. Jack Randall set off to walk back to . . . the other place, whatever it was—his place of lodging. He knew the way there through the woods.

With the new snow flattening sounds he felt almost deaf or dreaming. His boots crumped down into it. Two crows cranked past with their slow labouring stroke when a wind caught them and swept them round like a finger turning a clock hand. They rowed hard forwards and disappeared away to the side.

He punched the air again. That'll teach them. That'll teach them to try Old Jack Randall in the ring.

*　　*　　*

Back in his room, Jack Randall tried to tidy himself before slipping out again. He wetted and wiped his face. Without a mirror, he consulted his reflection in the window to see how damaged he was, pulling the curtain behind him to deepen the image. When he saw himself he laughed. His smile was wide, weird, undulating because of the flare of his lip. This made him smile more. His battered eye disappeared, closed behind a soft pink vulva of swelling that felt warm to the touch. At least he could neaten his hair and clothes. He scooped water onto his head and combed.

Margaret was standing in her favourite spot along the ground-floor corridor when she saw him walking towards her. This place was a small rounded recess with a high circular window so that her thoughts were accompanied by the sombre grading of the winter light through the day. The wounded man walked towards her, half-hiding his face, feeling his way with one hand skimming along the whitewashed wall. He was short, shabby, his face multicoloured and horrifying. Then, as in a play, she saw the doctor see him and call out, 'John! John. Where are you going?'

Jack didn't stop. Matthew Allen had to run after him and catch at his arm. John tried to whisk his arm away. Allen caught at him again and turned him around. 'John. John, good Lord, what has happened to you?'

Again Jack tried to whip his arm free. Doing so, he struck Dr Allen lightly on his temple. Allen

101

then lunged for him and held him in a hugging restraint, his arms pinned to his sides, Allen's hands locked together, squeezing into the softness of his belly.

'Unhand me! Unhand me! Blackguard, I'll knock you down. You think you're man enough for Jack Randall? Eh? Eh?'

'John. John, you are John,' the doctor panted. 'And you were warned that you couldn't stay away overnight. There will be consequences now.'

'Let go of me! I'll knock you down!'

'Mary! Mary!'

Suddenly Margaret wasn't just watching the pitiful play. The doctor was shouting and looking directly at her. She pointed slowly to her chest.

'Yes, you.'

'I'm Margaret.'

'Yes, Margaret, sorry. Can you call Stockdale. He'll be on the second floor.'

'I was out fighting!' John pleaded. 'That's all. It's an honest man's trade!'

'You'd been warned,' the doctor repeated. 'It'll be two days in the dark room.'

By the time Stockdale arrived the doctor was almost on the floor with John, trying to struggle out of his looped grasp like a drunken man trying to get out of his trousers. Stockdale intervened, securing John absolutely.

Margaret watched them drag the poor wounded man away to be shut in the dark.

Thrown onto the floor, the door slamming shut behind him, Jack Randall picked himself up and beat with his fists against its wood.

'Have none of you the pluck to come up to the scratch?' he roared. 'Blackguards! I'll take you all!

Starting with that mincing bottle imp doctor!'

Matthew Allen spoke back calmly through the shuddering door. 'John, you had been warned. It isn't possible for you to sleep out in the woods. You know you must return in the evenings.'

'Bastard! Shit-eating bastard! I'll . . . I'll . . .' He varied his rhythm and thumped the door with three spaced punches.

'John, you'll do yourself more harm. Just look at yourself.'

'Son of a whore!' Darkness covered him. He grovelled at the crack of light under the door.

'You knew the punishment, John. Two days.'

'You cannot cage a man. You cannot. I'll tear this door down!'

'I'll return later.'

'A light! Just please give me some sort of light!'

Dr Allen walked away down the corridor. Back among the other patients he was aware of John still shouting like a dog yapping at the gate, but after a few hours it ceased.

*　　　*　　　*

Beyond any sound of the mad, Hannah walked with Annabella and Muffet, her dog. The snow had shrivelled, was crusted in hollows or on the lee side of trees only. The forest was wet and stretched away in soft tapestry colours.

Muffet didn't like the cold. She trotted ahead, turning back with mute worried glances, eyebrows fidgeting.

'Oh, I didn't say,' Hannah went on. 'He was skating when I arrived.'

'Skating?'

'On his pond.' This detail had come back to Hannah in good time. She had finished the first avalanche of narration, telling it all at once, and in the silence just afterwards she was beginning to wonder if it sounded like anything at all. Annabella was reassuringly excited, though. She asked, 'Was he good? Did he "cut a dash"?'

'He was quite good, I think. I didn't see for very long. He stopped when he saw me.'

'That's good.'

Muffet had trodden on something. She stopped, stretched back a trembling hind leg, kicked with it, then carried on away behind a tree.

'So you spent all of the afternoon with him, talking?'

'About poetry mostly.'

'About poetry. That's very promising.'

'Yes. Do you think?' Hannah remembered the long glutinous silences and was embarrassed to mention them in case they were a bad sign. But she did very much want her friend's opinion and found a formula. 'He was quite . . . morose.'

'He's bound to get lost in thought at times, given what he is.'

'That's what I decided.'

'No, no. I do think this is promising. We need to plot something more. And I still haven't seen him.'

'We were together for hours,' Hannah said, feeling the thrill of it again, but striding casually, in a worldly way.

Spring

She sat in the light of the window and looked almost too frail to bear its blast. He could see her fingerbones sharp and yellow through the cracked skin. The dent of her temple looked like the result of some violence. The skin of her face had drawn so tight that her lips were pulled against the hardness of her teeth. There were welts of shadow under her eyes and cheekbones.

He was telling her that she needed to eat, that if she didn't he would be forced to feed her. Milk and custard, he was saying. Soaked bread. She could hear that he was exasperated, as with an awkward child, whereas it was his understanding that was childish. But she couldn't explain to him, the effort of speech made her head ache, and her voice seemed of late to emerge as a shock, a little live thing in her mouth, jumpy and peculiar. It had none of the smooth serenity it had in her mind. So she didn't tell him that to eat was to join the ordinary world of bodies and murder, of lust and destruction, was to swim through the world like a worm through soil, eating, making ordure. Possibly it was a thought he could understand, but what she could not begin to try and explain to him was that in Heaven to see and to eat are the same thing. Looking is absorption, is union, without destruction. There nothing is broken. Light flows into light endlessly, in harmony, and is perfectly still.

'You're smiling,' he said. 'I hope that's a smile of agreement. No recovery of animal spirits is possible . . .' Animal spirits! There was his stupidity in a phrase. He lived in contradictions he did not even perceive. '. . . although you don't yet lack energy to the point of ceasing to move, that will come unless you are less cruel to yourself.' He pinched the bridge of his nose, sighed through it. 'I have said all that I wanted to say. I trust it has been understood.'

Margaret inclined her head. Matthew Allen accepted it as all the response he was presently likely to get. He patted her hand, its few dry sticks, and walked back to his study. The Silent Watcher watched him go.

The drawing on his desk—its cleanliness, its power, its levers. It could make the whole asylum an irrelevance if he so chose, and that was tempting, but he would keep up both concerns and be finally the multifaceted man he was. He would flourish. The drawing was of a machine, a conception of his own, improving on past designs. The draughtsmanship itself gave him pleasure, a sign of his intellect. Sharp ink strokes joined at right angles to define a square, three-dimensional tiered object that stood in abstract white space. It had an angelic clarity. It would change his life. Not since his discovery of phrenology and the mental sciences as a young man had anything excited him so much. It was like falling in love, this profusion of harmonious thoughts, this coalescing of passion and possibility, this new life. Matthew Allen was deeply smitten.

He sat down and sobered himself with details. The two-tray system was clearly superior, with a tracer and drill connected in perfect symmetry. He lifted the drawing and laid it carefully aside. Today he would write to Thomas Rawnsley, the young man with the workshop in Loughton who fashioned machine cogs from hornbeam, and request an instructive visit to his establishment. Men of progress and industry conferring together, one of them a man of science.

He dipped his nib, shook away excess drops. 'Dear Mr Rawnsley,' he began. He looked up out of the window and saw the idiot Simon backing away in fear from Clara, who was scolding him for something. As she shouted she opened her clenched fists and shook out handfuls of torn grass. Matthew Allen turned back to his letter.

*   *   *

When Eliza Allen made the joke she held her tongue tip between her teeth for the moment after, as she always did, mischievously awaiting Hannah's reaction. Hannah looked away, blushing painfully, her skin swarming with heat. It wasn't as though the joke was even amusing; it hardly was a joke. Her mother's jokes rarely were obvious, hence that infuriating expression of hers while she stared around waiting. All her mother had said was why didn't she seek Mr Tennyson's opinion of the book she had in her hand. Hannah's discomfort was made acute by the thought of what it was she was reading. Had her mother read over her shoulder? Among her father's poetry volumes she had found an old Dryden and picked it out. Between the long, solid, dully rectangular poems in rhyming couplets she had found a song which began:

Sylvia, the fair, in the bloom of fifteen,
Felt an innocent warmth as she lay on the green.

This Sylvia 'saw the men eager, but was at a loss/ What they meant by their sighing and kissing so close'.

Hannah hadn't quite seen the men, or him, eager, but this was all very compelling.

> And clasping and twining,
> And panting and wishing,
> And sighing and kissing,
> And sighing and kissing so close.

This was one of the most explicit clues she had had as to what she might expect actually to occur when passions converged. The phrases, the little skipping tune, made her heart race. And sighing and kissing so close.

Hannah sat down at the table and ignored Abigail's protests as she tore a corner from the bread and butter the child was eating. She spoke over her. 'You have butter on your face, Abi. You are not a slice of bread, you know.'

Abigail appealed to a higher authority. 'Mama, she's eating my food.'

'Hannah, be kind to your sister. If you want bread and butter, there is . . .'

'I wasn't being unkind. I was sharing with her. Shouldn't she be taught . . .'

'Hannah, don't be contrary.'

'I'm not being contrary. I'm leaving.'

'Contrariness itself.'

'Not at all.'

The day was mild. Hannah let her shawl hang loosely from her shoulders as she walked to Annabella's. She pinched her cheeks as she walked onto the lane, in case of an encounter with him.

Annabella was in her garden, under the early blackthorn blossom, reading. 'Good morning,' Hannah called.

Annabella looked up, enhancing the scene, as she always did, with her beauty. 'Greetings, fair nymph. Isn't this tree heaven?'

'Yes, it is.' Hannah studied it with the appropriate dreamy appreciation. There were no leaves as yet, just slender black branches and the damp white blossoms ruffling in the breeze. The tree looked ardent, single-minded, standing there and declaring its flowers straight out of the wet, gnarled wood. 'Very pretty,' she said. 'Shall we go for a walk?'

'Has something happened?'

'No. The ordinary torments of the familial life.'

'I'll just go and tell Mama.'

Hannah stood alone until Annabella returned. Alone. The quiet garden. Annabella's life was so different to her own, just the one brother, her books and blossom and beauty. Sometimes Hannah, surrounded by her family and the mad, by all those hurrying or drifting people, felt as though she lived her life on a public thoroughfare.

As they walked, Hannah watched the effect of her friend's beauty on the people they passed. Did Annabella realise how much she lived in the tunnel of it, always enclosed within the circle of its impact? It aligned men, stiffened their backs, knocked their hats up from their heads. A farmboy leading three cows right now lifted his hat straight up, smirking at her. If Hannah had had that advantage, she might have been more sure of gaining Tennyson. It was a power at least. Hannah had no power. There was nothing she could do.

There was nothing any girl could do in choosing a husband for herself beyond panting and wishing and hoping, making herself visible, agreeable.

'Snowdrops,' Annabella said, pointing at a little group of the trembling white things. 'Shall we go into the church?'

'Why not?'

This was becoming a habit on their walks. The first time it had felt like trespass, secret and wrong, to enter the church in their state of lazy reverie and admiration. By now it had an element of ritual. They passed the leaning gravestones in melancholy silence without stopping as they had in the past to calculate the ages of the people when they'd died and pity the children among them. There had been one seven-year-old girl who had moved Hannah to the point of tears. She greeted her mentally now as she passed on her way into the cold stone porch. Reverently, Annabella pulled open the heavy oak door and they stepped inside. The door closed solidly behind them, shutting them into a silence that magnified their footsteps and made them take shallower, careful breaths. An extinguished atmosphere, the sense of snuffed candles, of a room someone has just left. Annabella crossed herself. Hannah did the same, and prayed by whispering the name Alfred Tennyson once without sound and with her eyes closed. Ardently, her lips formed the syllables and she breathed silently through them.

Annabella pointed to the flagstones where the sun through a stained-glass window cast a delicate circle of coloured floating light. Hannah nodded.

She walked up the nave towards the pulpit and stopped at the bronze eagle lectern with the big

Bible on its outspread wings. She looked at the page. *And in the sixth month the angel Gabriel was sent from God.* The elaborate large initial reminded her of her explorations of how beautifully the letters AT and HA could be calligraphically combined. Afterwards she had burned the page in the stove, her heart pounding, as though destroying the evidence of a murder. *To a virgin espoused to a man whose name was Joseph, of the house of David; and the virgin's name was Mary.*

She looked up. Annabella was seated in a pew, her lovely eyes upcast at the east window. Hannah joined her, sitting on the pew on the other side of the aisle. She lowered herself into the creaking wood and looked up at the glass, the stiff translucent figures around Christ on the cross, His handsome head lolling on His right shoulder. She looked at the muscles of His body, at His sadness, until she felt a genuine pity bloom inside her.

After long quiet, the church door opened: the warden, Mr Tripp. He crossed himself and walked into the vestry, glancing across under heavy overhanging eyebrows at the two girls apparently praying, and recognised the doctor's daughter and the pretty one. When he was gone, they looked at each other. Hannah pointed at the door and they got up and crept away.

*   *   *

John was no longer allowed out of bounds, not even to return to work in the admiral's garden. For that he had been replaced. His key had been taken from him. He could wander only within the grounds of Fairmead House and knew that he was being watched. It was his challenge had done it.

His few days in darkness had been a living death, but worse: without rest, without God, without ceasing. When the door was shut the room had started to sink down and down until it was deep underground, deeper than a mine. He could call upward to the surface, but no one would hear. When the door was opened again and he was freed at ground level, the coloured world had rushed howling in, into the vacuum of his starved senses. The force of it had knocked him on his arse. His head was too heavy to lift, his hands as feeble as leaves. He sat on the ground outside, feeling light hit the back of his head, the breeze swarming all over him, and stared down at the blades of grass between his thighs and one climbing ant until he could manage more. Later, he wondered if he was dreaming it all: he'd wanted the world back so much that maybe his crazed mind had made it for him and he was still underground. The clouds, the trees, the birds all moved so exactly as he knew they did.

After he'd regained himself, pieced the parts back together, he felt a terrible and righteous rage and John shuddered and faded and flinched while Jack Randall again took charge. The doctor he would never forgive, and there was no one from whom he would not seek redress. To proclaim this, he'd issued a challenge.

Jack Randall The Champion of The Prize Ring Begs Leave To Inform The Sporting World That He Is Ready To Meet Any Customer In The Ring Or On The Stage To

114

Fight For The Sum Of £500 or £1000 Aside A Fair Stand Up Fight Half Minute Time Win Or Lose He Is Not Particular As To Weight Colour Or Country All He Wishes Is To Meet With A Customer Who Has Pluck Enough To Come Up To The Scratch
      Jack Randall
   So Let Thine enemies perish O Lord

That was a while ago. He was mostly John again now, but still he couldn't go anywhere. He looked up at slow, steep-sided clouds. He held a fine twig at the end of a branch and looked at its tight triangular buds like an infant's tiny fingernails. He heard a woodpecker drumming out in the forest and felt distance tug at him. He pulled on the branch and let go so that it whipped up and bounced.

John walked to a bench. When he sat he saw that he held the Bible in his left hand and remembered why. He pulled out a loose paper from his pocket and spread it beside him to continue his work. The large, final words were calming to write. They resounded. They were heard.

Weep Daughters Of Israel Weep Over Saul Who Cloathed You In Scarlet More Fair To Behold . . .

*   *   *

There were feathers in the clearing, three of them, connected at their shafts, a scrap of torn wing. They stood on one edge, shuddering like the sail of a toy boat in the breeze. Around them the dark leaves and frail flowers of bluebells that glowed here and there where the sun struck through.

Margaret sat and heard the wind pouring in the leaves overhead. She had fallen in the river once, as a child, and heard the rushing deafness of drowning. But she had been saved. The flowing of the air around her seemed to intensify, to grow louder, until it was so powerful it reversed her breath. It almost lifted her from the ground.

The wind separated into thumps, into wing beats. An angel. An angel there in front of her. Tears fell like petals from her face. It stopped in front of her. Settling, its wings made a chittering sound. It paced back and forth, a strange, soft, curving walk that was almost like dancing. It reached out with its beautiful hands to steady itself in the mortal world, touching leaves, touching branches, and left stains of brightness where it touched. Slowly, unbearably, it turned its face to look at her. When it spoke, she felt that the words were spoken precisely in the middle of her mind, but that they somehow pervaded the whole forest. The leaves crisped and trembled. 'Do not weep,' it said. 'I am an angel of the Lord.'

'Forgive me,' she said. 'Forgive me. Forgive my husband.'

Inclining its head towards her, it smiled. 'There are things I must reveal to you.'

Margaret dared to look at it, hearing its voice quiet and full of love, and saw that angels' faces are subtler machines than human ones. There were parts that worked sideways as well as up and down. It registered the finest changes, momentary and delicate, as it moved, like the iridescence on a pigeon's neck.

'Is He . . . Is He coming?' she asked.

'Do not,' the angel told her, 'ask to see Him. His Love is a flood. His glory is a fire. You could not withstand it. And we have need of you. Hold out your hand.'

Margaret did as she was instructed. The angel dropped onto her palm something small and round, about the size of a hazelnut picked up from the ground. 'What is it?' she asked.

'It is all that is made.'

Margaret looked at it, marvelling at its minuteness, its delicacy. It had rivers narrower than a leaf's veins that pulsed, seas that ticked back and forth, and around it was the brightness of its own sky, then other skies, then darkness.

'Only because God loves it,' the angel instructed, 'can it exist. Without His love . . .'

'It vanishes.'

'Vanishes. Vanishes. Vanishes.'

The angel removed it from her hand. Looking up, Margaret saw how the trees stretched their arms behind the angel, to protect it.

'Here now is your first instruction.'

'I submit. Utterly, I submit.'

'Your name is no longer Margaret. That was the name given you by your earthly parents, used by your husband. Today you are rechristened.'

'Rechristened.' At that word all the leaves and trees were still, expectant, formal. She waited, not breathing for long heartbeats.

'Your name is Mary.'

'It is too much.' Margaret covered her face with her hands.

'It is His Word.'

'Mary,' Margaret whispered.

'Mary.'

'Mary,' Mary answered.

'Mary, you must bear witness. You have a task.'

'I cannot bear it. I am excrement, a husk.'

'It is His will. He has called you worthy.'

'I submit utterly.'

'Then you know what you must do.'

'What I must do?'

'Drive them out.'

'Yes. Yes, of course.'

'Now I will dance for you and shortly I will be gone. You will be left with your task.'

Mary sat and watched the angel dance. As it turned and twisted with joy, it touched the world, leaving brightness. Soon it was surrounded by the marks it made and danced in a wheel of obliterating light.

*   *   *

Hannah walked and recited the remarkable facts to herself—a poet, tall, handsome, strong, dark— and out of her thoughts he appeared. Under the bell of her skirt she stumbled, seeing him, but continued forwards, calm, preparing her smile. What would happen? In her mind, the apex of their next encounter was, outrageously, a kiss, his large arms around her and the fierce kiss kindling where their lips touched. He craned his head forward to identify the approaching girl, then lifted his wide hat.

'Miss Allen, is it not? I recognise the form.'

'Do you? It is. That is to say, I am. Good morning.'

He approached near enough to see her clearly

118

and talk without effort of his voice. Hannah caught the sharp reek of his body as he did so.

'You're carrying a book,' he told her.

'Yes, indeed.'

'And what book is it, if I may ask?'

'Certainly you may. It's . . .' she lifted it and read the spine as though she had forgotten. 'It's Dryden, Dryden's poems.'

'You don't find him too dry, then?' He laughed at his own joke, appealing to her to do so also. She tried to and did, perhaps a little vehemently, to reward his friendly intent.

'And may I ask,' she said into the amicable silence, 'what you are reading at present?'

'You may, you may. Also poems, though with less pleasure, I imagine. My own. I'm preparing a volume.'

'Oh, that's wonderful.'

'Is it? I don't expect the critics will agree with you. If I ever publish it, I expect they will treat it no more kindly than my previous efforts.'

'Critics, they're . . .' She had no strong idea of what they were, so raised her arms disparagingly. 'They're critics. They aren't poets. And I certainly look forward to reading it. Perhaps you might inscribe a copy for me. It's very exciting to have a poet here, aside from Mr Clare, that is.'

'Mr Clare?'

'John Clare. He's a patient of my father's.'

'John Clare, the peasant poet? I see. That's . . .' Tennyson frowned. As he did so a small cloud slid away from the face of the sun. Colours deepened. The little pebbles glinted in the path. A breeze lifted the branches.

'That's better,' Hannah said.

'Hmm. I can do that, you know. Would you like to see?'

'How do you mean?'

'Stand still and watch.'

Tennyson approached even closer so that Hannah was inside his sharp smell. Was this it? What was he about to do—kiss her? Hannah stood absolutely still and closed her eyes also to receive the pressure of his lips. But it didn't come. She opened her eyes again to see Tennyson with his eyes and mouth firmly closed, pursed shut. So he hadn't seen her close her eyes. That horror of humiliation had not happened. She breathed deeply. Tennyson stayed as he was for a moment. Then, very gradually, he relaxed the muscles of his face until it was as expressionless as a death mask. He continued the outward movement, slowly opening his eyes and mouth, and opening them more, until his eyes were startlingly wide open and he smiled broadly with his eyebrows raised.

Suddenly, as though a fit had ended, his face dropped back to normal. 'There it is,' he said. 'The sun coming out from behind a cloud.'

'It's . . . remarkable,' Hannah said. She wasn't sure what it meant to be chosen to see this performance. Was he being avuncular, treating her as a child? Had it not occurred to him at all that she might presume he was about to kiss her?

'It's a party piece,' he explained. 'I used to do it for my friends at Cambridge.'

'Oh, yes.'

'Yes. Arthur Hallam. Well, he . . . I shouldn't detain you.'

'That's quite all right.'

'No, no. I should be getting back. Good day to

you.'

'Good day.'

Tennyson tipped his hat and walked back into the murk of thought about his dead friend. Hannah watched him go, his long legs loosely hinged at the knees. Things she might have said clamoured within her. Nevertheless, they had just met alone and talked, and he had smiled and entertained her. There was good reason to hope.

Summer

A quickening in the leaves. Bright clouds. People working in the garden.

Mary stood in the rush of the day and watched them. How they suffered as they went about their tasks, muttering to themselves or instructing the air, laughing at nothing, shaking their arms, twitching, rocking back and forth, closing their eyes suddenly and holding still like a child awaiting a blow, like a wife awaiting her husband's fist. They were attacked, all of them; devils attacked them. Her truth would exorcise them. But it seemed that Simon was safe. She watched Simon, so large and soft with his big white hands. His coat was pulled smooth as a horse's hide across the breadth of his shoulders. His curly hair shivered in the breeze. He was not the first person she had to give the news. Somehow, in his idiocy, he knew. He was kind and frightened, and magnified the kindness in others, shamed their cruelty. More was not required of him. Look how he tended the vegetable patch with his watering can. The thick leaves purred and bounced under sparkling strings of water.

The pure water. Drops scattering. Seeds of light falling in the grass, on the earth. She made light, also. She must have caught it from the angel. Her fingertips left stains of golden brightness that she struggled always to leave in threes or multiples of three. She had to speak. She couldn't keep it in. As though her mouth were full of water. But to whom?

There was Clara, a witch, a friend of the devils. But not Clara. Not yet.

125

William Stockdale approached on his rounds. In his hand he carried a stained cloth and so she knew that he was the one she must try first. She could not see whether the stain was blood, but it was certainly ruddy, dark, human. He was Roman, a crucifier. He held the people in torment. She stepped into his path, held up her hands and he came towards her, not knowing that he had no choice but to come to her. He didn't see the shining tunnels in which people walked when they moved according to His Will. No matter. She stood still and he was brought to her.

'The Lord is love,' she began.

'Indeed,' he said, not stopping.

'He is love,' she repeated, stepping again into his path, halting him. 'And He is everywhere.'

'That's nice for him.'

'And returning. He will return and He will judge.' She tried to stare piercingly up into his eyes, but the sun burned behind the man's head. She addressed his waistcoat buttons. 'You must shrive. Your soul is in danger. You can hold nothing back. All is seen.'

'I've seen plenty myself, and if you don't mind I've work to do.'

'Take heed. Hearken unto me. I bear an angelic message.'

'I'm grateful for the warning. Now if you'll let me ...' He stretched out his left arm, placed it past her shoulder and tried to sweep her aside, but she gripped him, swung round like a door. She must see the change in him. The word must reach him.

'You must be pure. You must empty yourself.'

Stockdale dropped the cloth onto the ground and with his free hand shoved at her forehead. Mary

126

flew back onto the grass. She smiled up at the sky and its finely dragged high cloud. Suffering had been sent her. She felt his gratuitous boot sink into her stomach. Her work had truly begun.

*   *   *

Annabella was good with Abigail, soft-eyed, patient, able to play. The child stood entranced, trying to keep her wriggling fingers still as the beautiful older girl wrapped around them the thread of a cat's cradle. Dora sat nearer the light of the lamp, embroidering borders on the linens of her future married life. Hannah had taken the finest needle from Dora's sewing box. Carefully she pushed it into the skin of her fingertip and across, then out of the other side, making a white ridge where it passed through. It wasn't painful, slightly tight, but not painful. She enjoyed lightly terrorising Abigail by showing her the sliver of metal passing through her flesh.

'Look, Abi.' She wagged her finger over Abigail's eyes, then grabbed her own wrist and sucked in air as though in pain.

'Ow!' Abigail said.

'Don't be so childish,' Dora said.

Hannah pulled the needle out again, placed it back in the box.

'I saw Mr Tennyson the other day,' she announced, not at all childish.

'Indeed?' Annabella raised her eyebrows.

'Yes, I did. We had a most pleasant conversation.'

'Did you? Hannah, why haven't you told me about this? No, you need to pinch it there and

127

there.'

'Can't,' Abigail complained. 'You do it.'

'But it's on my fingers.'

'You ought to be careful with your pleasant conversations,' Dora warned. 'You don't want to be taken lightly.'

'Why would I be taken in any way? We met in the lane. We spoke.'

'Hmm.' Dora examined her stitches.

'Has he heard you play the piano?' Annabella asked.

'Yes. That would be bound to induce a proposal,' Dora said.

'No, he hasn't. How could we arrange that? Take no notice of Dora. She is merely disappointed that her proposal has already come and it was from James.'

'I would be very happy with such a proposal,' Annabella said appeasingly.

'Neither opinion terribly interests me,' Dora said, smoothing the edges of a napkin.

'Here.' Annabella hooked her fingers through the thread, pinched and lifted from Abigail's fingers a neat crossed frame.

'Knock, knock,' said a voice. A loose bunch of wildflowers appeared beside the door frame, then, smiling beside them, the face of James. 'Oh,' he said. 'There are lots of you.'

'Don't be frightened,' Hannah said. 'Come in.'

'Don't be impertinent,' Dora chastised. 'I'll put those in water.' She got up, took the flowers from him, received with demurely downcast eyes his kiss on her cheek, and left.

'So,' he said when she was gone.

'Do sit down,' Hannah said.

He nodded and sat with a breathy smile in Annabella's direction, squinting as though her beauty were sunlight full on his face. He bent forward and patted Abigail on the shoulder; she looked at him and turned away.

'Those are your linens,' Hannah said.

'Are they?' he asked and bent forward to touch them.

The sight made Hannah shudder. It was precisely what had to be avoided: the life with linens, the dreary, comfortable, tepid life. She said suddenly, almost to punish him, 'And will you be happy, married to Dora?'

'I . . . I . . . well, what a question. Of course I will. Mutual regard, a marriage founded on warm mutual regard . . .'

'I thought so,' Hannah cut him off. 'I'm sure that you will.'

Dora returned with the flowers in a jug. 'There,' she said. 'James, you look very warm. Are you ailing?'

Hannah snorted.

'Is Hannah being impolite?'

'Impolite is a very strong word.'

'I thought so. Hannah, why are you not capable of being just ordinarily civil?'

'I am civil. You weren't even here.'

'Evidently. If I had been, perhaps you would have behaved in a less . . .'

'Less? Less what?'

Abigail cringed close against Annabella's skirt, holding the fabric with one hand.

'Or perhaps if you hadn't been here . . .'

'Oh, that's fine. That's really fine. I shan't be here.' Hannah stood up and fled the room.

Annabella, in the pained silence, fitted the cat's cradle again around Abigail's fingers, then got up and followed.

*   *   *

'Look at that,' Matthew Allen said to his son. 'Marvellous.' He bent forward with his hands on his knees, peering.

'It's a Maudsley,' Thomas Rawnsley told him.

'Oh, I know, I know. I've studied all the designs. It's simply that I haven't really seen a table engine working before.'

The hypnosis of its movement, silent, balanced, rhythmical. The viscous thrusting of its arms, well oiled. And the turning of the triangular centrifugal governor at the top, back and forth, like a girl hearing her name and turning towards him, saying Yes? Yes? Yes?

'This type of engine,' Rawnsley said, 'would probably suit your purposes as well as mine. I use charcoal, which is of course abundant here with the forest.'

'That I have already decided,' Allen told him, 'having studied all available specifications. But I haven't yet told my son what my purposes are.'

'It's true, he hasn't,' Fulton confirmed, wincing as the man working the drill filled the air with its screaming. 'So what is it?' he asked his father.

'Look around you. All the materials are here.'

Fulton did look around at the piles of squared wood, some of it still with the natural roughness of bark on its back or along its edge, most of it squared out of nature and geometrically regular. He looked at the tools, the sweet-smelling dust, the

130

display cabinet of variously sized wooden cogs, the boxes filled with the same. 'We're going to make machine parts also?'

'No, no. I wouldn't want to compete with our friend Rawnsley here,' Allen smiled. 'No, think.' He paused, then announced, 'Mechanical wood carving.'

'Like this?'

'I just said not like this. No, for furniture. Domestic. Ecclesiastical fittings.'

'It could well be a success,' Rawnsley commented, who already knew of the scheme. 'The market for mass production—not inconsiderable.'

'I see,' Fulton said.

'You don't seem quite as enthused as I expected you to be,' Allen told his son. 'It will make you rich. Think of all the new churches in all the cities. And think of all the people unable to afford fine furniture hand-carving, but who can have the same, of the same quality, carved to guildsmen's standards, because they are simply perfectly exact and precise mechanical copies of hand-carved originals, for a fraction of the price. That beauty and dignity, that elevating spiritual environment, made available to great numbers of people.'

'I see.'

'You see, you see,' Allen grinned and swiped a hand down his beard. 'A little investment and it will take place. Il aura lieu.'

'More difficult than producing these things, but plausible,' Rawnsley said, dipping his hand into an open box of tiny cogs, 'entirely possible.'

Matthew Allen also dipped his hand and scooped up a few cogs in his palm. They were warm still

131

from the machining and felt nutritious, like nuts. He liked Rawnsley, liked the prosperous sheen to his hat, his fine-checked trousers tightly strapped under his boots. 'Perhaps you would care to be one of my lucky investors?' he asked.

*　　　*　　　*

Stands in the wilderness of the world, stands alone, his face from his own house, a book in his hand, surrounded by strangers, trembling, unable, the sun heating him, his will breaking inside him, until he bursts out, 'What can I do?'

As though it were possible, he searches again the strangers' faces to find Mary or Patty or one of his own children or anyone, but there is no warm return from them. They are alien, moulded flesh only, and they frighten him.

A jarring of magpies overhead. He turns. He breathes. He is in a garden. He knows where he is. So why can't he stop it, why can't he kill it in himself, the sense that at any moment he might see her, that she might come for him, a door in the world swing open and there she is? That she might end this for him? *John, you have a visitor. John, you have a visitor.* The phrase repeats inside his head, endlessly, boringly, because he craves it, that she might come and end this for him.

Something tugs at the corner of his vision. He looks: a rising, a thing of the summer season. He walks over quickly to see. Like the plume of steam from a kettle's spout, ants are rising from the sandy hole of their nest. He crouches, his belly softly crushed behind his knees, and peers at the glittering black bodies swarming up to the surface,

132

raising their heavy transparent wings, flying up. He looks up at those already airborne. They hold mostly together, a cloud of them funnelling and warping in the wind. They fly beyond limits. He gets up and follows them as far as he can.

They disperse along the line, flaking off into clear air. Some land on the trees. He stands by one, in the cool wood-scent of its shade, and watches a single ant walk along a leaf. A breeze flips its platform, but it adheres. Many leaves shine against the light, the sweet, living green. He quotes himself under his breath. 'Leaves from Eternity are simple things.'

Ants fly over, carry beyond him. He can't follow them further. Like a lock gate opening in a canal, the water slumping in, his heavy rage returns. He presses himself to the tree, looks down and sees the roots reaching down into the earth. The admiral's hands. He has them himself for a second, thick, rooty fingers, twisted, numb. He shakes his hands and they're gone. They reappear at his feet, and clutch down. The painful numbness rises, his legs solidifying, a hard rind surrounding them, creeping upwards. He raises his arms. They crack and split and reach into the light. The bark covers his lips, covers his eyes. Going blind, he vomits leaves and growth. He yearns upwards into the air, dwindling, splitting, growing finer, to live points, to nerves. The wind moves agonisingly through him. He can't speak.

Stands in the wilderness of the world.

*   *   *

Dr Allen found the company he was in highly

congenial. Thomas Rawnsley had brought him along to an informal gathering of the area's industrialists, brisk and cheerful, ambitious and duplicitous men. They ate beef and the spiced foam of roasted apples. They drank beer. A light rain petalled against the windows. Pipes were smoked. Rawnsley turned out to be quite a different man with drink inside him. His stiff exterior was broken up and he emerged boyish and excitable, red-faced, clumsy and loud-voiced. He showed off his new acquaintance to the small crowd and implored him to hold forth on his scheme, which Matthew Allen did readily. He drew assent from them when he spoke of their great good fortune in having the forest at their disposal, with the charcoal burners to render it down to useful fuel and their own imaginations to turn the timber into anything at all. Tanning and ship building were old occupations. The new was up to them. Seated at their centre, Matthew Allen felt he easily outclassed them all, gifted as he was in so many respects, so educated and already a published author on chemistry and insanity. He was reflected back to himself in their smiles, their interested gazes. For a moment he heard his father's voice in his own, holding forth among the Sandemanians. When he had finished his description of the Pyroglyph there was even applause. Rawnsley picked up the jug and sloshed more beer into his glass.

*   *   *

Alfred Tennyson walked to loosen his blood. He had spent the day sunk in a low mood. The word 'sunk' was the right one, the mood soft, dark, silted, sluggish; it smelt of riverbed, of himself. He'd managed no new lines. Poems lay around half-formed and helpless, insects droned in the garden, a fly butted its hard little face against the window panes. He'd sat and smoked thickly enough to make his stupid head light with it, his heart flutter, his limbs feel shaky and hollow. Distantly he heard the rhythmic clubbing of woodmen at work among the trees.

The doctor might be a comfort. That man always had energy, afflatus, interest.

He passed among the tired lunatics and up the path to the doctor's house. He pulled on the bell and turned and watched a madman flinch and talk at nothing until the door was opened. A servant had opened it, but immediately the doctor hurried towards him, hand outstretched. He took Tennyson's larger hand in his own and shook it warmly, patting him on the shoulder as he drew him inside. 'How splendid of you to stop by,' he said. 'Come in, come in.' Tennyson handed the servant his hat and cape. The doctor led him in.

Mrs Allen met him in the vestibule. From a doorway, the youngest child veered out and clung to her mother's skirts. 'How lovely to see you again,' Eliza said. 'Do come through to the drawing room.'

From that farther room music started. Hannah had heard his arrival and rushed to the piano, her cheeks freshly pinched, to be accidentally discovered playing a Clementi sonata. She stumbled on a phrase as they entered the room, her face starting to burn. Abigail ran to her side, arriving with a soft thump against the stool, and

135

began to plink at the highest notes. Not daring to lift her head—she was still being accidentally discovered—Hannah pushed Abigail away with her forearm. The child tripped; her upflung arms were caught by her mother. 'Oh, I'm sorry,' Hannah stood up.

'No, no, you were playing beautifully.' Her mother smiled.

'Mr Tennyson,' Hannah said, 'what a pleasure to see you again.' Suddenly she remembered to be afraid: had he told her father of her solitary visit to him all that time ago? There was no sign of it that she could see. Perhaps her father knew and didn't mind. He was in one of his enthusiastic moods anyway, meeting everything headlong, with pleasure, his movements large and rapid. He looked delighted to have found her in the drawing room; he wore the warm, suffused, small-eyed smile of paternal pride. She was part of his achievement. To the benefit of her own desires, she would be shown off to their guest. 'That was delightful, Hannah. Would you play us something else?'

'If you are sure . . .'

'Of course we are.'

Tennyson made a gruff noise of agreement.

'Alfred, please take a seat.'

'I shall call for tea,' Eliza whispered and walked away. Hannah refused to meet her glance; she felt it needling at her forehead. She sat again and began another of the sonatas, but immediately thought of what was happening, who was listening: the tempo crumpled, notes clattered into one another. She shouted at herself in her mind to be calm, to play as usual, and even as she felt sweat prickling on her upper lip she regained control. She slowed through sweet phrases, held them up in display. She played on, only making further errors when her mother returned to the room with Fulton and Dora, and Tennyson lit his pipe. It was difficult also to look as well as possible while concentrating and knowing that her face had reddened in that awful flecked way it had. Through her closing bars the tea arrived. She played the final cadences with great vehemence and separation, then stood up feeble and helpless, her face slippery with sweat.

'Wonderful,' her father congratulated her.

'Very eloquent,' Tennyson said.

'Really?'

He nodded, exhaling smoke from his nostrils. 'Indeed,' he said.

The word hotly pierced her. Eloquent! And from a poet. She must have touched his soul! She now sat triumphantly among them and looked at her warm fingers while Tennyson went on with the thought that all young ladies ought to be musical, that it brightens a home. He asked Eliza if she played.

'Not as much as I used to, with so much to attend to. Dora plays also.'

'Ah, yes,' Matthew leaped in. 'And she will be brightening her own home soon. Dora is to marry in, what, just a couple of weeks now. I hope you will do us the honour of joining us for the wedding. The party will be here.'

'Well, yes. Why not?' Tennyson turned with courtesy to the silent Dora. 'I would indeed be honoured.' Such a thing, a lively and happy family. It was a pleasure for him to be among them. It was life as it ought to be lived, unlike his private, stagnant whatever you may call it.

The wedding, Hannah thought, would be ideal. What better, more conducive day could there be? It would happen! He had practically announced it himself. With her eloquent music, she would brighten his home.

Tea was taken while the conversation continued, light and cheerful and without hesitation. Tennyson ate a noticeable quantity of toasted tea bread and, slightly to Hannah's dismay, relit his pipe while still chewing.

When tea was done, Matthew announced, 'Ladies, if you will excuse us. Alfred, perhaps you would care to join me in my study. There's something I'd rather like you to see. Fulton, you too.'

'Certainly,' Tennyson said, and, along with his host, rose and bowed to the ladies.

'Good bye,' Hannah said.

'Good bye,' he answered. 'And thank you once again for playing.'

With an arm held out in a curve around his shoulders, Matthew Allen edged around Tennyson and guided him to the door. Fulton followed them, satisfied at being invited to leave the irrelevant women behind.

'Now, you may recall a conversation we had some time ago,' Allen began, softly closing his study door behind them, 'in which I expressed a desire to broaden the scope of my activities once more.'

'Indeed, I do. A most agreeable conversation.'

Allen smiled. 'Well, I believe that I have been inspired with just the sort of idea, one that is absolutely ripe for the moment, with truly remarkable prospects. Fulton, would you bring the drawings from my desk.' Allen picked up a mineral sample, tossed and caught it as he spoke. 'These are my designs. I am convinced that they represent the best of current thinking in these matters and, though it's not my intention to flatter myself, may represent a significant advance. Certainly the scheme is in advance of anything currently operating.'

'This is all very intriguing,' Tennyson said, sitting up as he received from Fulton the pages. He peered closely at the first. 'It's a machine.'

'Indeed. A machine,' Allen repeated the word as if he'd come to love it. 'A machine. A machine of my own devising.'

'The Pyroglyph,' Tennyson read. 'Odd bit of Greek. Fire mark. Marking what?'

'Wood. It is a wood carver,' Fulton piped up. His father checked his interruption with a glance.

'Precisely. A machine for the carving of wood. A Pyroglyph. Here,' Allen stood beside Tennyson's chair and pointed at the workings with his nugget of rock. 'This is a tracer. It follows the design of a piece that is carved by hand, by a master craftsman. This arm connects it across to a drill piece that carves the design exactly onto a fresh piece of wood fixed in this tray. The craftsman's carving is reproduced so precisely that it is impossible afterwards to tell the original from the copy. Here on this sheet, some designs.' Tennyson looked down a page of curling leaves, diamonds, crosses, eggs and darts, cherubic faces. 'The implications of this? Well, just think of them, think of all the homes in our growing cities unable to

139

afford the work of guild craftsmen, now able to afford indistinguishable examples. There is, let us not forget, a moral enhancement that comes with living with fine design, in wood. It connects people to the natural world and to English history. And think of all the new churches also unable to afford teams of craftsmen to decorate them . . .'

Tennyson felt the surge of Allen's articulacy passing into him. The doctor's enthusiasm was positively galvanic.

'Fulton, would you excuse us for a moment?' The boy looked at his father as if to check that he really meant it and then, in the silence, left.

Now was the moment for Matthew, the crucial manoeuvre. He seemed to have Tennyson in a receptive state.

'Now,' he began again, 'the project is in a very advanced state of realisation. I will shortly be investing all of my savings in the building of the Pyroglyph and purchase of its engine. However, that still leaves an amount of capital required for materials, premises and so forth.' Tennyson did not seem to betray any dismay at the turn the conversation was taking. Allen pressed on. 'So my hope is that you will consider investing in the scheme along with me. I already have a site selected. Everything, in fact, is primed and ready to go.'

'It sounds most convincing,' Tennyson said. 'No doubt the market exists. The cities . . .'

'Oh, I'm quite sure the market exists.'

'And as it happens, I have money. We all do. An inheritance from my father.' Money that could be active in his place, flowing through the world, returning increased. Tennyson could join with the doctor and himself become a man of enterprise, of energy.

'Well, I would sincerely ask you to consider it.'

'Consider it considered.'

'You mean to say . . . ?'

'Dr Allen, I would very much like to buy a share in the Pyroglyph.' Tennyson held out his hand. Allen grasped and held, forgetting in his excitement to shake it.

'That's wonderful. Quite wonderful. I'm . . . I really am delighted. Now, shall we consider some sums?'

* * *

Mary's mouth was tired. She felt as if she'd spoken for days, for weeks, her spit thickening to a paste, her tongue always lifting and falling to spread the Word. She had lost the ability to sleep. At most she experienced a quick splash of black in the depths of the night before waking again, already praying and speaking. As she walked, the world bulged towards her, close and particular, full of signs. She walked in her bright tunnel from person to person, from soul to soul. It led her now to the pond where John stood.

John stood and stared down at the widening hem of slime where in the heat the pond had shrunk down into itself. A thick smell to the heavy green water, a sexual stink. It looked oily, frog-coloured. He was about to crouch and see if he could see through its reflections to the creatures living within when he felt a hand on his shoulder.

'Good morning,' she said.

'Yes,' he said. 'Yes? Who are you?'

141

'My name is Mary.'

'It can't be.'

'It is my name, given me by an angel of the Lord.'

'Yes, but you look—I suppose we are—older. We couldn't escape it, could we?' He reached up and touched her face. 'Oh,' he said. 'Oh.' Mary smiled. She had his attention. She could see he was ready. The contact was deep and sincere. 'I knew you'd come,' he said.

'Of course.'

'But you're thin.'

'I have something to tell you,' she said.

'Let's go somewhere, somewhere out of sight. We can hide, be free together.'

'Listen . . .'

'Ah!' He startled her by crying out. 'Why did you take so long?'

'God's will,' she said. 'We must not question it.'

'Yes, yes. But it's been so hard.'

She saw tears in his eyes. 'I'm here now.'

'Ah!' he cried again. He picked up one of her hands and held it to the side of his face, comforting himself. 'Come on,' he said. 'Before they find us.'

He kept hold of her hand and led her away. He hated to harry and assault her, but it was so urgent, they might have no time at all. He pulled her after him away from the house to the walled yard where the grass clippings were dumped and vegetable trash was left to compost. There he grabbed her into his arms and crushed her against him. She permitted this. She felt the thirst in his soul. She had been sent to help him. 'It is the Lord that has sent me to you,' she said.

'Yes, yes. It must be.'

His hands now chased over her back, over her

142

hair, her shoulders, her buttocks.

'No,' she started. 'No, no.'

'Yes. Finally. We're together now. This is right.'

Was it right? Was this a sacrifice she had to make, the penance of life with her husband revisited upon her? She wished to be entirely an instrument of the Lord. Was this a way?

The man's ardour was overwhelming. She found herself on her back on the moist grass, its odour of sweet rot. John lifted her skirt, tugged at her underthings. Her body belonged to the world, after all. It would fall, would decay. She closed her eyes. Her Silent Watcher kept vigil.

John pulled at his own buttons. He kissed her face, her eye, the hard bone in her cheek. He worked and found the place. 'Mary,' he said. 'Mary.'

She kept her face screwed tightly shut, feeling his face bumping against her, his tears on her cheeks.

He rocked on the pulsing sensations, inhaling the grass, the gold day resting softly on his back. He pressed in. He was older—his belly made a soft barrier between them—and her bones were so sharp. He pressed down into her until it broke from him, the lightning that forked down into that darkness and branched and spread. He whimpered and hugged her to him. 'Mary,' he moaned and rolled off her. She tried to get up, but he held on to her, keeping her there, and she submitted, pressing her face into him instead, burrowing into the darkness of his neck. His head pressed into the musky, damp grass. He felt the warmth of her tears falling onto him. Her hair lay across his face, across his mouth. He looked up. Transparent flaws circulated in his vision. Two flies buzzed, battling

143

together. Swifts screamed overhead in the glorious summer heights. 'Mary,' he said again in his happiness, slowly closing his eyes.

*   *   *

Tennyson's money was quickly banked, premises were rented, quantities of oak, lime and hornbeam were ordered, and the Pyroglyph was put into construction. Matthew Allen walked among the screaming drills of the place where it was being born, enjoying all the wrenching power of manufacture. He'd had the exhilaration of new ideas before, ideas that had altered the shape of his life, established him in the world, but he'd never seen an idea being built, bodied forth in space, hammered together.

He hired two men, one thin with long capable fingers and fingertips so large his hands looked like a waterbird's feet, and one square with slow pale eyes, both former hand-carvers for cabinet makers and both untalkative. The square man flexed his hands, staring at them, and asked in a manner that indicated his disapproval about the lack of apprentices. Dr Allen reassured him that operating the Pyroglyph would not require training to that standard or, happily, the same amount of labour. Once the patterns had been carved, the work would be light and pleasant. The date of their first day of employment was agreed and Allen was left alone in his empty workshop, enjoying the taut convexity of its silence, regarding the as-yet-unfired Maudsley engine. So much was on the brink of occurring. He locked the premises and went home to draw up further advertisements.

144

Matthew Allen's powers of immersion were prodigious. Like a sea mammal, he disappeared down into his new element for hours. He surfaced, was loud and cheerful and hungry, and then vanished again. Fulton tried to follow him—this was work he would share and inherit, after all—but he often couldn't find him. Eliza was occasionally irked that this should be happening so close to the wedding, but she did not complain; she knew it wouldn't avail and anyway she was more than capable herself.

William Stockdale's imperturbable strength and slow-moving control encouraged Allen to give him more and more of the regular running of the asylum, particularly at Leopard's Hill Lodge. He admired, for example, how Stockdale dealt with John Clare, who now walked towards them down the long corridor.

Stockdale looked down at the addled peasant who attempted to fix him with his pale eyes. He explained who he was—Shakespeare—and that he spoke seven languages. He boasted and then suddenly was angry. 'Where's Mary?' he demanded. 'What have you done to her? She came for me and now she's gone.'

Matthew Allen interrupted him. 'John, John, wait. Mary has not been here. You desire her so much that you've imagined it. Do you understand?'

John turned to him with no understanding in his expression. 'I didn't imagine it. It was too real. It was real. What have you done with her?'

'We haven't done anything with her,' Stockdale said. 'She hasn't been here.' He stood over the man, gripped his shoulder. 'She hasn't been here. Do you hear? Do you hear?'

'Don't . . .'

Stockdale shook him gently. 'She has not been here. She has not been here. Do you hear?'

'I . . .'

'You see, you do understand.'

'Let go.'

'You do understand.'

'I understand.'

Afterwards, Stockdale confided. 'It's not force, but a physical impression. It commands their attention, doctor.'

*　　　*　　　*

At home, Allen rushed upon little Abigail and grabbed her up into his arms, gnawing on her belly. She kicked and exulted. He dropped her down. 'Oof,' he said. 'You're growing too big for such things. Now, ladies,' he addressed his wife and daughters. 'New dresses have been ordered, as requested. They will arrive tomorrow, I understand, easily in time for the wedding.'

'Will they?' Hannah swallowed against the pain in her throat. 'What has been ordered?'

'I'm sure they will satisfy. Your mother made the selection, from magazines.'

'Indeed, I did,' Eliza said.

Hannah fervently hoped that her dress would be of the right shade, something with twilight in it, with distance and poetry. She swallowed again. Her throat was sore. A scratching dryness kept tunnelling down inside and she had to swallow to soothe it. Her bones felt heavy, her vision heavy also. She looked around in slow swerves. She was falling ill. She would be ill for the wedding. The moment she admitted it, she sneezed and afterwards groaned, her head ringing.

Dora looked disapproving. 'I hope you're not planning to be ill for my wedding. You should leave, Hannah. We can't any of us catch it from you.'

*　　　*　　　*

'It might have been Arthur and Emily getting married. If you squint it almost looks like them. He has the same brow, I think.'

'Declarations in the yellow drawing room,' Septimus answered.

'And then he would have been our brother. The dear endeared.'

'Might have been. Would have been. Enough of the conditional mood. Only the possible happens.'

'Only the possible happens? Can that be true?'

'Take it or leave it. What difference?'

'I can't bear it, you know, sometimes, I can't . . . bear it.'

'Yes.' Septimus fell silent and waited for the profound moment to blur and dissipate. Then he said gently, when his thoughts had moved on, 'He was good for her, certainly, roused her from her sickbed.'

'And now she will marry that garrulous midshipman. What a falling off was there.'

'Are you playing Hamlet? Arthur was wonderful. It is unlikely that our sister would find someone as wonderful again. She hasn't.'

'You're being very rational.'

'I'm too tired to be anything else.'

The two Tennysons with their wine bowed at new

guests. Hannah watched them do it. She was ill. She stood in her stiff new dress, which was too brightly blue, with aching knees and elbows, patting the sweat from her forehead and upper lip with a lace handkerchief. Around her the wedding party shifted and droned. She stared thickly at Dora and James seated at their little table with spiced cake and wine, receiving the compliments of standing guests. They looked isolated there, immobile and cut off and child-like, being shorter than their guests. To Hannah it seemed a humiliating position to be in, made worse by Dora's unsuitability for the ringlets she wore. They were left out of the party. Everyone else knew their business and were freely able to enjoy themselves. Perhaps she would have felt differently if they had looked happier. But they weren't laughing or gay at all. They spoke only when spoken to. They didn't hold hands. Hannah turned to Annabella to comment on this, but found instead her uncle Oswald and his small brown wife.

'Good day to you,' he said. 'Your father has made a splendid occasion of it.'

Hannah swallowed and answered. 'Indeed.' She could hear her father's loud laugh in the background, his public laugh, theatrical and rhythmic, not at all similar to the sound of his real amusement.

'Such fine wine,' Oswald said, holding up his glinting glass of Madeira. In her illness, Hannah found its swaying jewel colour very absorbing to look at. He lowered it again.

'Well, you know Father,' she said.

'Yes, I do. No expense spared.'

'Such a lovely dress,' Mrs Allen said, reaching

148

out and touching the crisp bulk of Hannah's sleeve.

'Thank you.' Hannah patted her forehead again with her handkerchief.

'Are you quite well?' Oswald asked.

'Not quite.'

'Your father should have said something, I could have brought a tonic.'

'Oh, Annabella, there you are.'

'Yes, here I am.'

'Uncle Oswald, allow me to introduce my friend, Annabella. Annabella, this is my uncle and aunt.'

'Very pleased to meet you.' She curtsied.

'And you,' Oswald bowed. His wife dipped slightly, whilst sipping.

'Will you excuse us, Uncle?'

'Of course.'

Hannah and Annabella walked apart with linked arms.

'I feel dreadful,' Hannah said.

'You're very warm.'

'This sun is too bright.'

'But is he here?'

Hannah tried to look into her friend's eager face, but her white dress was such a mass of blooming light that was too much for her. She wiped her face. 'Yes. Haven't you seen him with his brother? They're so much taller than everybody else.'

'Which one is he?'

'What? He's him. The handsomer one. The hair.'

'Oh, yes. He is dark, as you said.'

Hannah felt a throb of fear at what she had to do and was almost too weak to withstand it. It was now, it was today, in this place that she would talk to him. She had to gather the strength to do it.

'Shall we go over to them?' Annabella asked.

'I suppose,' Hannah answered, but was saved by the arrival of her father. He took Annabella's hand and held it out to the side, admiring her with a smile.

'How lovely,' he said. 'You must come and meet the other guests. I think more or less everybody has come. The Carlyles have sent their regrets, but there we are. Come. You too, Hannah.'

Hannah followed after them. She watched where he stood without looking at him, as an animal knows where the farmer stands.

Boxer Byron heard the voices and hobbled towards them on his sore club foot. He saw them, he saw what they were doing, making a travesty of living love. He could see the couple, bound together felon-like with the harsh bindings of the law, seated among the people who had taken Mary from him. He quickened towards them, rolling his shoulder as he limped.

There were attendants between Fairmead House and their garden, he saw, to keep him away, so he stood at a distance and watched, waiting until one was distracted. A little girl child ran up to one and gave him cake. The man followed after her for a few yards. Byron hurried through the gap.

He barged into the drifting people and sought the doctor, declaring so. The doctor made himself known.

'Where's Mary?' he demanded.

'John,' the doctor said. 'You should not be here.'

'Where's Mary?'

'Now is not the time or place. You will have to leave. This is my daughter's wedding day.' He beckoned to an attendant.

'Your daughter? And mine is Vicky, your queen.

150

So what do you have to say to that? I demand your obedience.'

'John, you have to leave.'

'Under what compulsion? Obey me. Where's Mary?'

'John . . .'

Byron saw the dead no in the doctor's face, the shut door, and tried to punch it. He missed. The doctor stepped forward and tried to hug the poet's arms to his sides while the people stared. Byron worked an arm free. From someone's plate he grabbed up a piece of cake and in his rage crushed it so that its currants and sweet paste fell from between his fingers. He tried to fling the rest into the doctor's face and wipe his fingers onto his smug expression. The doctor shut his eyes and leaned back. Then William Stockdale was upon them. He grabbed Byron's arms and lifted him for a moment entirely off the ground. He set him down and yanked an arm up the poet's back, twisting his bones.

'Please take him away.'

'Happily, doctor.'

'To Leopard's Hill Lodge . . . simply deteriorating and deteriorating . . .' Smoothing his clothes, he turned to his guests, avoiding Dora's hard stare. 'Nothing to fear,' he said. 'Nothing to fear.'

Charles Seymour stood apart with the self-assurance of rank. He leaned back after the commotion had subsided, head cocked on one side, idly spiralling the wine in his glass and smiling faintly at the other guests. Hannah was despatched by her father, who had assiduously courted his presence, to speak to him. Annabella also he

151

encouraged to converse with the young heir. No doubt, he told her with crude gallantry, she could charm him. Hannah was annoyed. She had failed to talk to Tennyson and the minutes were dribbling away. Also, she was no longer feeling even nearly fresh or attractive. She must have looked damp, pale, half-blind, fussing with her handkerchief and squinting. Then, as they made towards Charles Seymour, Tennyson passed closely by, and Hannah, falling now into the crater of the moment, said, 'Mr Tennyson.'

'Ah, yes,' he replied. 'Good day to you.'

Annabella squeezed Hannah's arm, and did so again until Hannah understood.

'Allow me to introduce my friend,' Hannah said. 'Miss Annabella Simpson. Mr Alfred Tennyson.'

Annabella curtsied in her graceful way, lowering her chin as she sank down, then raising her countenance upwards as she straightened, softly smiling. 'Indeed,' Tennyson said, and advanced his face close to hers so as to see her clearly. He spluttered with an embarrassed laugh. Then he stood tall and said, 'And what sort of creature are you—nymph or dryad?'

Annabella giggled. 'I'm afraid I am merely mortal.'

'To judge from your appearance, it seemed in order to ask. Beautiful day, no?'

Of course, of course. Hannah wiped her forehead. She let them talk on for a moment more, then pinched Annabella's arm. Annabella turned and looked into her friend's red eyes and understood.

'If you would excuse me,' she said, 'I must go and speak to Mrs Allen. I haven't done so yet. She

152

must think me terribly rude.'

'By all means.' Tennyson bowed.

Hannah smiled. It was over, she knew. It was already over. The failure was outside of her body. It was already there, in the green and sunlit day. And it had always been there. In every thought she'd had about him, or just behind it, was the emptiness, the hollowness, the knowledge that she was wrong, that it wasn't true, that it wouldn't happen. The realisation came as a great liberation. Weeks and months of prayer and hope suddenly evacuated from her. She could say anything and her words would just be air, unavailing as a fragrance. She might as well tell the truth. Sweating and faint, she was nevertheless calm. The world was thin around her, bright and threadbare, and she spoke out loud what she actually thought.

'Mr Tennyson,' she began.

'Yes?'

'For a long time now I have wished to say something, to know something.'

'Is that so?'

'It is. You see, I have developed a great admiration for you. Well, it's more than that. I'm enamoured, might be a good word. And I was hoping that this admiration might be mutual, that you might perhaps consider me as a possible wife, a plausible wife.' She laughed at the phrase.

'I see.'

'Yes. Absurd, isn't it? I shouldn't have said anything. It's very unconventional, but then I thought you aren't conventional. Also, I have a fever.'

'I see.'

They stood there together with the people

moving around them. Tennyson said nothing for a long time. He exuded his familiar, thick silence, then said, 'I'm very honoured, of course . . .'

'Of course,' Hannah laughed.

'But . . .'

'Please don't feel you have to finish that sentence. I've been most tiresome. If you would excuse me. I'm very sorry.'

Hannah smiled and turned and hurried into the house to be sick.

Annabella found her when eventually she returned to the garden. 'Well?'

'No, not well.'

'Frankly, I think you'll live to be relieved. I mean to say, are all poets so dirty? Did you see his ears?'

'I wasn't especially looking at his ears.'

'A lucky escape. You can think of it thus.'

'Oh, I will. Who wants to be married to such ears?'

Annabella's disrespect was typical and did not at that moment upset Hannah, although later it would remain in her thoughts. Annabella's beauty fronted for her; behind it she was disloyal, satirical, and nobody knew. 'Nymph or dryad?' She tried to mimic his Lincolnshire accent. 'Nymph or dryad?'

Posthumous to hope, Hannah felt quite empty apart from the seethe of her sickness sensations. The one effort she still had to expend was to make sure she was always where Tennyson was not. And soon the day would be over. Days ended, like everything else. She chatted as best as she could with other guests and allowed her damp hand to be kissed when her father introduced her to the brightly dressed Thomas Rawnsley, who made machines or something else and lots of money. It was only later, when she was alone in her bed, that she cried and cried.

* * *

'Pssst!'

Eliza looked up from her household accounts. 'How may I help you?'

'Shh!' Matthew pressed a finger to his lips, then beckoned with a curling finger to follow him through the doorway.

Eliza blew on the inked page and went after him, found him loitering half-way round the corner of the vestibule. When he saw her, he moved on. She laughed, bustled after.

'Where are you leading me?' she called.

He crouched out of sight. When she rounded the corner, he stood up, pirouetted, and beckoned her on.

'Fool.' She followed him, laughing as he danced away.

The house was empty, with all the wedding guests gone. He led her all around it until she was panting, then finally stopped by his study door. 'If you would care to follow me.' He smiled. His whiskers looked mischievous.

'Gladly,' she breathed.

He opened the door for her and in she went. She saw immediately what he'd been leading her towards.

'What is it?'

'Aha,' he said. 'What is it indeed?'

Eliza looked at the box on the floor. 'I thought it was one of the wedding gifts when it arrived.'

'In which case you were wrong. Isn't it beautiful?'

It stood on his desk, a brass machine with three curving feet, a stem, a barrel with a handle and many radial arms that branched up at right angles with finer stems surmounted with globes of different colours, some of them surrounded by a corolla of tiny globes on separate stems.

'It is called an orrery.'

'Heavenly bodies?' she asked.

'Of course. The sun there in the centre.'

'It's beautiful. Was it very expensive?'

'What a vulgar question. Come here, my dear, and turn this handle.'

'I won't break it?'

'Fear not. The heavens are at your command.'

He stood behind her and held her waist, warmed by the chase through the house. Eliza took the handle and turned. The mechanism was beautifully, gelatinously smooth. From left to right the worlds revolved with their moons waltzing around them while the large brass ball of the sun stood unmoved, adored, reflecting the lamplight.

'What is the one with all those moons?'

'Jupiter.'

'Aren't you clever?'

'Terrifically. Prodigiously.' Matthew kissed her neck.

*　　　*　　　*

The day was light and taut. A breeze hissed against the trees. High white cloud was dragged across the blue. She could smell the burnt dust of the path. There had been no reprisals, not yet, for her sin, no claws pouncing into her, no shame. She was in accordance with His will. There was yet work to do. The exorcism was reaching its climax. She closed her eyes and prayed.

A voice said, 'Too frightened to look, is it?'

Mary opened her eyes and saw the one who she had been waiting for, Clara, the witch. Mary thanked God for sending her. 'I have no fear of anything. You are the one who fears. Everywhere you see . . .'

Clara giggled. 'You are a liar,' she said. 'I can do things to you.'

'No, you cannot. I am invulnerable because . . .'

'Yes, I can. Terrible things. You couldn't invent them.'

'I'm alone in a madhouse. I've nothing but His protection. What can you do? You have . . .'

'You think this is the worst? You think this is the worst there is?'

'I know there's worse. I've known it. Most of us have. I've spent hours . . .'

'But being Jew-Jesus's whore, you're preserved.' Clara giggled again.

'God loves you too. It is limitless. It is larger than this world. This world is so tiny . . .'

'I'd piss on it.'

'It's there. Even after you've pissed on it, it will be full of kindness, radiant . . .'

'Why don't you show me? Why don't you come with me? There's something I want to show you. If you can stand it.'

'There's nothing you can show me . . .'

'Then come and look at it. Come on.'

Clara started walking away, her hair twitching over her shoulder. Mary paused only for a fraction of a moment, then followed. Death could take nothing of value from her, so what could Clara do?

Simon trotted over to Clara to ask her where she was going. He grabbed hold of her shoulder. She dived away out of his grasp and turned on him.

'But where don't you . . .' he began.

'We're going to the place,' she whispered. 'You can't come.'

'No . . .' he lowed.

'You cannot come.'

Simon knew not to try to disobey her. He put a finger in his mouth and stood back.

Clara led Mary to the gate. Peter Wilkins awakened from his seat, pushed his hat back on his head and unlocked the gate for them.

They immediately left the path. Clara stepped over brambles, the broken light flickering over her. Things flew. The forest made its little eating sounds.

'A little further,' Clara said.

A clearing of scraped earth. There was something on it.

'Here. Now look upon it.'

'You dwell in darkness and there is no need. Light is abundant. It searches out every part of you. It loves you.'

'Shut your holy, stinking mouth. This is my place you're in. Look upon it.'

'What is it?'

'It has powers.'

'It has none. It has no connection . . .'

'Shut your mouth and look upon it.'

Mary stepped forward and looked down. It had the form of a circle and was about the size of a large plate. It was beautifully made from tiny pieces. At its edge was a fence of small sticks. It had a spiralling, repetitive pattern made with feathers, remarkably matching stones, berries, insects' shiny wings, nuts, leaves. At its centre was the swirl of a snail shell. Mary looked up at Clara who was smiling, muttering, apparently waiting for something to happen to Mary, for her to be distressed, changed in some way. Again Mary looked at it and felt her gaze absorbed. She found it pitiable, with that safe house of a shell, that dream of home, at its centre. Intricate and powerless.

'Now that you've seen it,' Clara told her, 'the demon will have entered you.'

'No demon can enter me. An angel told me so.'

'What you invent is your own affair. Wait now and see.'

Mary shook her head. She felt nothing. Perhaps the exorcism had already been achieved. Clara was mistress of no devils. To be sure, though, Mary set her foot on the shape and dragged it across. Clara ran and knocked Mary onto her back and tore at her. Mary, in a moment of dreadful, unchristian weak-mindedness, put up her hands to defend herself. It pleased her then to have those hands bitten and stamped on. Clara spat finally on her and ran away. Mary felt burning trenches in her face. The trees swayed peacefully over. She stood up and cool blood poured down along her chin. She caught drops in both hands. She stood and held her hands out until they were bathed. She pressed her hands to her face, printing them scarlet, and walked triumphantly back to the madhouse.

There she met William Stockdale, who took a relishing look at her and said, 'Oh dear, oh dear. I think the doctor will have to see about this. Time,

I'm thinking, you spent some time at my pleasure in the Lodge.'

Autumn

'Listen, listen, we'll make a penny or two, what? Old days, nothing. I know the public's taste as well as I ever did.'

He stared at him, stared into him, but he could see in John's eyes that it wasn't John looking out, or was only for fractions of moments, when he would sense himself seen and look quickly away. John was speaking very rapidly. In the middle of his fattened face, his mouth was dry and muscular, his breath unclean.

'There's a Doctor Bottle imp who deals in urine
A keeper of state prisons for the queen
As great a man as is the Doge of Turin
And save in London is but seldom seen
Ylcep'd old Allen—mad brained ladies curing
Some poxed like Flora and but seldom clean
The new road o'er the forest is the right one
To see red hell and further on the white one.'

He wanted to be out of that cell. It was a nightmare, simply a nightmare—his old friend mad and gabbling and laughing as he read from a greasy notebook. It was like a possession. And the air was rank. And there were noises from other chambers.

'Earth hells or bugger shops or what you please
Where men close prisoners are and women
    ravished
I've often seen such dirty sights as these
I've often seen good money spent and lavished
To keep bad houses up for doctors fees
And I have known a bugger's tally traversed

163

Till all his good intents begin to falter
　—When death brought in his bill and left the
　halter.'

　　　　　*　　　　　*　　　　　*

John Taylor walked back from Leopard's Hill
Lodge with Eliza Allen under the fragmenting
trees. Thin puddles split beneath their feet. Leaves
flowed down around them.

'A sibyl's prophecies,' he said. He was upset by
what he'd seen, by the dwindling lives of his
friends. This classical thought now set a seal on his
mood and slightly assuaged him.

'I beg your pardon?'

'A sibyl, a prophetess,' he explained. 'She would
write her prophecies on leaves and let the wind
scatter them, read them who can. I spend my time
now in ancient studies, mostly Egyptian, the
pyramids and so forth.'

'I see. You should tell my husband. I'm sure
he would be interested. But how did you find
Mr Clare?' she asked.

'Not well,' he answered. 'He was . . . agitated. He
kept asking after his childhood sweetheart, Mary. I
hadn't the heart to tell him that she has died.
Also—it would be amusing if it weren't the index
of quite appalling suffering—he seemed at times to
be under the impression that he is Lord Nelson.'

'Oh. Sometimes it is Byron, I am told.'

'That makes more sense. He's rewriting one of
Byron's poems. He also spoke very violently,
obscenely in fact, against the place and your
husband, whom he says he hardly sees at the
moment. He showed me part of the poem

164

"Don Juan", where these sentiments were also expressed. How long has he been in there, rather than Fairmead House?'

'I'm not exactly sure. More than a month. Many patients do spend time there when it is necessary and return later. And as to my husband, John Clare can hardly have seen him, he is so busy with the wood manufactury.'

'You didn't know him in his pride, I suppose. You can only have seen him distraught.'

'I am used to seeing people distraught.'

'But you should have seen him as I knew him.'

'His intelligence is still evident.'

'Intelligence I'm not so sure about. I mean, no doubt he has a good deal and he was always very astute about people. But the height of his powers, his inspiration—it was something to behold. He lacked rhetoric. He lacked shape and used many unfamiliar words of his own dialect. But the living earth, the world he knew . . . if you will permit me an extravagant formulation, it sang itself through him. England sang through him, its eternal, living nature. Thousands and thousands of lines, and all of it fresh, seen, melodic, real. It was genius, absolutely. How can that power be destroyed, he asks, knowing there is no answer. Excuse me, I simply wanted to think of him then for a moment. You said, didn't you, something about your husband's manufactury?'

'Yes, the carving machine.'

'Oh, of course. The Pyroglyph. A fine Greek name a sibyl would have liked: the fire mark. He wrote to me on the matter. Unfortunately, I'm in no position to invest at the moment. So, he's all taken up with that, is he?'

'Yes. In his headlong fashion. Not to say that he is neglecting the asylum.'

'And how are you, Mrs Allen? It has been such a long time since I saw you last.'

John Taylor had a certain dry charm, Eliza remembered, appropriate to a literary man, a bachelor, and a scholar. She associated genteel, well-kept rooms with him. In their clean silence she imagined she'd hear only the scratching of a pen or the eager, quiet sound of pages being cut.

'Not since you brought John.'

'No, longer, my dear. I saw only your husband then. And your son. Is that correct? No, it was when I published your husband's book. Some years.'

Eliza smiled. John Taylor regarded her face, softly ageing, handsome in the flaring autumn light.

'And are you well?' he enquired.

'I am. We prosper, I suppose. We are all in health. Dora is now married and lives not too far away. There is the wood carving.'

'Your husband isn't neglecting you for it?'

'No, no. We both have much to do, I suppose. You must come now and see him.'

'Indeed, I must. I have to settle John's expenses.'

'We have guests you might like to meet. Perhaps you have already. Do you know the poet Alfred Tennyson?'

'I'm afraid I'm not much concerned with poetry any more, but I have heard of him. He's here, is he? I'm afraid the reviews have chewed him about a bit. They've grown no kinder since my poor Keats suffered them. I hope he hasn't been crushed. He's a patient?'

166

'No, no. His brother is. A melancholic. In fact, the family are here visiting; they comprise the party. No, Alfred is heavy for spells, I understand, but not deranged.'

They turned off the path and towards Fairmead House. They found the party at tea. Matthew Allen was standing, a cup in his hand, holding forth to a party all younger than himself, mostly women, two of whom were examining a piece of wood. He broke off when he saw the publisher, greeting him with his eyes while he finished the sentence.

'Mr Taylor, what a pleasure. Do take a seat. Fulton.'

Fulton obediently stood to offer his own seat.

'Oh, no. I'm afraid I can't stay. So you're Fulton. You have grown.'

'Thank you,' Fulton said and looked down, embarrassed at the stupidity of his answer.

'Allow me to introduce you. John Taylor, these are the Tennysons.'

'A number of them,' one mumbled.

'Alfred Tennyson you may have heard of. Alfred, this is John Taylor, erstwhile publisher of Keats, Hazlitt, Lamb, our own unfortunate Mr Clare, and, I suppose I must confess, one of my own works on the classification of the insane.'

'I have heard of you,' Taylor assured Tennyson, who had risen to shake his hand. 'You have been called cockney, I know, and compared to Keats.'

'I'm not much of cockney, being from Lincolnshire, but they accuse me of similar sensuality and indolence, as they see it. They do me too much of an honour, did they but know it. It is an honour, of course, to shake the hand of a friend of Keats.'

'I was honoured to know him.'

Alfred Tennyson was tall and dark with lengthy limbs, a wide-mouthed bronze face and large hands. Taylor, comparing him with his dead friend, saw a different languor, a kind of tired ease about his presence that was unlike Keats, but there was a similar something—the gravid silence, perhaps. But not Keats's quickness, his darting anger.

'You are with Murray, aren't you? They are a very good house. I hope you will produce more. You must not let the magazines discourage you in any way. Theirs is a barbarous form of coffee-house entertainment. Yours is infinitely higher.'

Tennyson heard the voice of an older generation in that 'coffee-house'. Encouragement from this older man who'd known real poets was welcome. 'I thank you for those words. I don't think that they will stop me. There's really nothing else I'm fit for. Do you still publish poetry?'

'No, I'm afraid I could not make it pay. The public's taste has moved on to useful works and prose novels, as you know. But poetry will survive. Civilisation has never been without it.' Taylor's eye was caught by the flash of a brilliant silver teapot of fashionable design. Evidently what Eliza Allen had said was true: they were prospering. 'It won't pay, but it will survive. We want it, at least. Now, on the subject of payment, Dr Allen, would you favour me with a moment of your time.'

'Certainly.'

'It was a pleasure meeting you.' He bowed to the company.

Tennyson watched him leave. A small man, not particularly smart, with a tired, kind face, but a friend of immortals, a survivor of poetry.

With her hope blasted and withered and unexpected tears not impossible, Hannah had intended not to like the Tennysons—she wouldn't have been there at all if Father hadn't insisted—but she hadn't succeeded. The ladies were clever and distinct, sharply characterful and expressive, particularly the beautiful older sister Matilda, who might have put Annabella in the shade. Her fascination was only enhanced by the fact that she walked with a slow, semicircling limp. And when they spoke about their home, it sounded like the warm refuge she'd always imagined for herself, full of books and animals and invented games, with no patients and no business on the premises. Abigail had liked what she'd heard also, especially the idea of having a pet monkey and a big dog pulling Mother along in a carriage. She had immediately requested a monkey from Papa, who had laughingly refused as though the idea were ridiculous and he wouldn't even think about it at all. There were enough of them to look after a monkey. It would be amusing. Hannah tried not to look at Tennyson. She had convicted him of indifference and then the susceptibility to Annabella that affected even the stupidest people, but she could not, of course, entirely extinguish her feelings for him. Disdain twisted painfully together with yearning. She looked at the tablecloth. She sipped her tea.

Matthew Allen returned to the party with Taylor's money safely stowed in his desk. He liked handling money, liked possessing it, but the more potent and secret pleasure was risk. There was a pent force in having things at stake that seemed to charge one's limbs with energy and made eventual

169

triumph more intense than could be imagined. This dream had been the cause of his early imprisonments in the past, but look at him now with his buildings, his patients, his distinguished reputation, and orders already accumulating for machine-carved wood. He held the new teapot high above his cup and poured a long, musical arc. By the end of the afternoon he had all the other Tennysons investing, except Septimus, whose nerves were to be spared the strain of capital adventure.

*　　　*　　　*

John felt the warmth of a hand on his shoulder. He knew its touch, its weight. 'Patty!' he said, turning.

'I thought you was all alone,' she said. 'It's dark in your room, ain't it?'

'It is dark. I am alone. Just that tiny window. Stars and clouds, never a bird or living thing. In hell. I'm alone in hell, Patty. At night, in darkness, doors get opened. Things happen.'

'Hush, now. Don't you want to know of your children?'

Patty sat down beside him on the hard, sour cot and pulled his head onto her shoulder, a strong and comforting woman. Her heavy cool fingers held his brow. She pulled him into the smell of her. He snaked an arm around the soft curve of her belly and grasped the cloth on the far side of her waist.

'The children are well,' he said. 'I know they are. They're free. John carpentering for the railways. Charles a clerk to that lawyer. Anna Maria to marry. I want to come home.'

'Why do you want to come home? The people aren't free there either.'

'They're not shut up. They're not locked away.'

She shook her head. 'The land is fenced. Can't walk across nothing. We're kept in narrow tracks. The common land is owned. The poor are driven away, the gypsies also.'

'The rich man is a tyrant and we are all prisoners. No one cares for the poor. They can burn ricks and riot. Nothing. Transportation. A whole continent is made a prison for them.'

'You're safer here.'

'No, I'm not. At night . . .'

'Shh. There's someone here to see you.'

Mary approached the bed.

'You! But how did you get in? Through the walls?'

'What are walls?'

John laughed. 'In your innocence you don't know.'

While Patty held him, Mary approached, the beautiful child, barely taller than him seated, and kissed him, a flake of gold that fell spinning into his mind.

'Sit beside me,' he said. 'Sit beside me. Now, here we are.'

Between the two women, John sat, his two hands joined with theirs rested in his lap, linked.

'We're together,' he said.

The flow between them, kindling smiles from each other, their gazes touching, until John felt a warm drop on his right hand. Blood, branching immediately into the tiny channels of his skin. He looked up, saw the small wound beneath Mary's left eye.

'Oh,' he said.

'Why did you do this to me?' she asked. 'I was ever gentle.'

'I was a child,' he protested. 'I never meant. You were so pretty in the orchard. I wanted to touch you. I felt so far away. That's why I threw the hazelnut.'

'Look. My face is healed.' The cut closed as he watched. Her skin resumed its placid surface like water.

'It's beautiful.'

Mary smiled back at him for a long moment. She held his gaze. She radiated love.

'Do you miss your sister?' she asked.

John felt his face crumpling. 'Yes,' he said. 'And nobody ever asks.' Along his side he hurt, frost-bitten, scoured by the winter wind, exposed.

'They don't know of her. Barely she glimmered in this world. You didn't know her.'

'She was a baby, my twin. Where did she go?'

Patty explained. 'Into a rich man's coffin. She died before baptism. She had to be snuck into holy ground.'

'So she's safe. But she would have been here. We would have loved one another.'

'You say that,' Patty said, 'but you were a solitary child, dreamy and distant.'

'Cause she wasn't there!'

'Here she is,' Mary said, and placed into his hands a sleeping baby. Closed purple eyes, curled fingers, a blunt, breathing nose, a soft swirl of hair. The warm weight of her head lay in his left palm.

'This is her,' he said. 'This is my sister.'

He looked up at Mary and Patty, disbelieving, overcome. When he looked down again, he held in his hands a bird's nest. He didn't recognise the type although he knew them all from his egg collecting. It was light, springy, tightly woven. Nor did he recognise the eggs. There were four of them.

'There we all are,' Patty said. 'Better now.'

The eggs were white as bone china. They glowed, tender and natural, lightly resting against each other.

'There we are,' he said. He lifted the nest and the eggs rolled with the irregular, delayed movement they had when there were chicks inside. 'There we are.'

*   *   *

'It's this part here that's the trouble.'

'This frame.'

He nodded in his infuriatingly slow way and said no more, so that Matthew Allen had to ask, 'And what is it that's wrong with it?'

'Being made of wood, even within the iron frame, it's soft, too soft. It don't hold it tight, and then because it's loose . . .'

Matthew looked again at the product. The carving was scribbled, all jittery scratches and ragged gashes. The clean, deep design was lost. He looked down at it and in his rage felt the power that would have bitten down and carved it perfectly, the will that barged and bullocked inside him.

'And they're all like this.'

Again that slow blink.

'Well?'

'It's this part here. They's all going to come out

173

the same. Course I could finish them by hand, tidy them up.'

'No, no, no. Obviously that is not how we're going to go on. The whole point, the whole scheme, is mechanical wood carving.'

The terror of risk was that while it charged Matthew Allen, had him skimming into the future with a harsh exhilaration that felt like delight, while it filled him at every moment with the sense of his own possibility and power, if it failed, if it failed all that rushing energy simply crashed like a carriage into a ditch and there was nothing, there was humiliation, debt, imprisonment, and all that he had defied would be all that there was. That was the risk. He threw the board across the room with sudden force so that his employee jerked back and, like a nervous old woman, placed a hand over his fluttering heart.

'Damn it to hell!' He calmed himself, running his hands down his beard. 'Then this part of the machine must be remade in steel. That is all there is to it. Orders will be delayed. But there's no alternative. Very well. Very well. I'll get to it instanter.'

'What shall I do? I can finish a few by hand.'

'No, no. What did I say? No, you go home to your wife.'

The man smiled slyly. 'I don't have a wife.'

'Then you can change your clothes and go out looking for one.'

'Oh, I've had interested parties. Will I still get paid?'

'Yes,' Allen hissed. 'Now go. Things are suspended here for two weeks at least, I imagine. I shall let you know.'

As he walked back to High Beach from Woodford, Matthew Allen composed in his head a letter to his customers of such persuasive excuse and finely phrased affirmations of the historical import of the enterprise, along with the irrefutable truth that revolutions are not made in single days, that he had restored his mood by the time Thomas Rawnsley appeared beside him on his horse. He greeted the younger man as one manufacturer to another. He even alluded to the day's difficulties and was cheerfully condoled by Rawnsley, who knew all about such technical vicissitudes. Rawnsley, when asked, revealed that he was in fact riding towards the doctor's residence to pay an impromptu call. He wished to offer a gift of apples from his garden. Would he find the doctor's wife and daughter at home?

*   *   *

From her window, Hannah could see Charles Seymour prowling outside the grounds, swishing his stick from side to side. Boredom, a sane frustration, a continuous mild anger: Hannah thought he looked like a friend, someone whose life was as empty and miserable as her own. Clearly he needed company. She went downstairs to meet him. It didn't matter now; she could meet whom she liked, and she was very bored.

When she did so, he raised a hand to lift his hat and found that he wasn't wearing one. He smiled and mimed instead. Hannah gazed for a moment down at his shoes and smiled also.

'Good day to you,' he said.

'Good day.'

She looked up at him again. He had a froth of fair hair and a smooth, beardless face that was colouring in the wind.

'Chilly today,' he said.

'Indeed. The weather is from the north. My father says this aggravates the patients.'

'But your shawl looks warm.'

'It is.'

His imagining of her physical state was pleasing. It was gentlemanly, aristocratic, to assume this curatorial intimacy with people. Of course, he was an aristocrat. To be his wife would be to be raised up in society and made secure. Absurd thought, and she wasn't thinking it for herself. And he was passionate. Hannah knew that he was there sane, against his will at his family's insistence, to liberate him from an unwise love. So they had both been denied their loves.

'I'm feeling dull today,' he said, swishing his stick again, in a tone that suggested he might tell her anything, that he was honest and unconcealed. 'I must admit it. First of all, I've finished the book I was reading. It wasn't terribly interesting in the first place.'

'My father has a library. I'm sure he'd give you use of it. And I have quite a few books.'

'Well, that's kind of you. Your father stocks a library for all of us, but it tends rather to the devotional.' He tapped his stick against his boots as though taking guard to play cricket. 'To be brutally honest, I'm not a great consumer of literature. I think some distraction is all I'm looking for.'

'We could go for a walk.' He looked up at her and immediately she added, to dissipate the effect,

176

'At some time.'

'I trust you don't go walking with any old lunatic? I'm not mad, you know.'

'Yes, I know.'

'Hmm. You are bored as well, aren't you?'

'I . . .'

'Good afternoon. Well met.' Her father's voice. She was discovered. And with her father was the young man Rawnsley.

Charles answered for both of them. 'Good afternoon to you. I'm Charles Seymour,' he said, extending his hand to Rawnsley.

'Thomas Rawnsley.'

Matthew Allen smiled at the three of them, his child and the wealthy feudal relic, who'd been too stupid to invest in the Pyroglyph, greeting the energetic industrialist. Rawnsley bowed to Hannah. She felt him trying to hold her gaze as he did so. There was a heaviness of meaning in his look, of questioning. She didn't know what it meant and wondered if the others had noticed, but they gave no sign of it. Charles Seymour continued the conversation.

'Your daughter just suggested to me . . .' Her heart bumped. '. . . that you might be kind enough to allow me use of your library. I could do with the entertainment.'

Matthew Allen thought that typical. 'Entertainment, no doubt,' he answered, 'and instruction. It would be my pleasure.'

*   *   *

The exact same weight of dark.

It was a source. Out of it flowed that time. He

177

himself flowed out of it, a youth, a child really, as he had been when he had woken in this exact dark.

He walked out back then, into that time, a lad under stars with the excitement beating inside him. Come gentle Spring, ethereal mildness come. He stumbled as a cart rut gripped his boot. He had a headache but without pain; the fierce expectation made his head bones light, his skull noticeable under thin skin. He wanted to cry out and sing, but had to be secret.

In the darkness of the stables the horses whinged and shifted. John spoke softly to them. He kept a calming hand flowing over their flanks as he walked around them, then soothed their heads towards him to throw over and fit the halters. The horses had to be out early this time of year to graze themselves full before the flies woke to torment their eyes and twitching skin.

He led them out, stumbling quietly behind him. They pulled against him, then obeyed as he led them to a different field where the other boy earned his halfpennies watching two other horses. As he unfastened the halters John called to the other boy in the dark.

'Over here,' he answered.

John jogged over, handed Tom the halters.

'And what you promised.'

John had them ready in his handkerchief, separate from the rest. 'One penny for watching them and one for not telling.'

'Where're you going?'

'I'll be back before they have to go back.'

'But where?'

'Stamford. Doesn't matter.'

'To a shop, is it? Buying ribbons for a girl, is it?'

Hearing the horses already cropping the grass, John set off towards the town. Come gentle Spring, ethereal mildness come. And from the bosom of yon dropping cloud, While music wakes around, veiled in a shower of shadowing roses, on our plains descend. That was where he was going. He didn't know why, but the first time he had read these words, in the tattered copy of Thomson's *Seasons* the visiting weaver had allowed him to see, his heart had twittered with joy. On our plains descend. The weaver had laughed at his transports, his sudden breathlessness. The weaver was a Methodist and rated Wesley's hymns far above Thomson's bucolic pentameters. His copy held only half of 'Autumn'. All of 'Winter' had flaked away. John desperately desired his own volume. He bothered his father for money unrelentingly, hoarded his own pennies, and finally gathered enough.

The bookshop was empty, its blinds down. John sat staring at it in the empty centre of Stamford, listening to a dog bark. He loitered like a thief, hands in pockets, the words dancing along his nerves. Come gentle Spring. Picked up and blown off course, still a child, obsessed by a few words and not knowing why. He sat and waited and almost felt he ought to hide when the owner arrived and unlocked his premises.

He watched until the man had lit his lamps, light softly blooming inside the window, then knocked at the door.

'Yes? I'm not open yet.'

'Sorry. I'm sorry.'

'What is it, lad?'

'I have to go, you see, back home. Can you sell

me Thomson's *Seasons*? I have the money already exactly.'

'Ah. Oh.' The man looked about him as if searching for an excuse, but couldn't find one. 'Very well, very well. Poetry, is it? Give me the money, then.'

'Yes, yes.' John scooped the coins out of his pocket and poured them into the man's hand.

The owner, who within a few years would be publishing John's first poems at a profit, stood and counted slowly while John danced from foot to foot as though needing to relieve himself. 'It is exact,' the man said. He opened a box and parsed the coins into its compartments, then finally took the volume from a table and handed it over.

'Thank you,' John said. 'Good day to you. Thank you,' and hurried out under the sprinkling notes of the bell.

As he walked back towards Helpston with the book in his hands, not daring to open it until he was somewhere safe, the dawn started to come up, wide and coldly dazzling and raw.

He lay and watched through his window the same ascent of strengthening light.

The maze of a life with no way out, paths taken, places been. He heard his door unbolted, saw a wooden plate of food shoved in.

*   *   *

She lay on the floor of her room and tried to bear it. She could hear them all, could hear the devils in this new place shrieking as they rioted in their hosts, but there was nothing she could do, locked in this foul room. She was exhausted anyway,

180

spent, an excremental husk. No brightness was left by the touch of her fingers.

She lay in her open grave, miles down, with the sharp voices of the place like dim clouds far above. She lay as still as she could. Her heart kept up its hateful slow tread in her chest. Warm tears that gave no relief now and then rolled into her ears, stopped, started again. Ever so slightly, she moved her hands, closed her fingers a fraction and felt the joints creak. An event: her hands' minute twitch like something killed. She felt killed. Everything felt final. She was covered in death as with a thick paste. She lay at the bottom of this well, stinking of death, on dead wood, enclosed within dead walls, but she wouldn't die. Everything was terminal and nothing ended. God kept His Presence from her. Unimaginable that it would be otherwise. The idea would have pushed a laugh out of her mouth if she'd had the energy. There was nothing else. Just the empty light moving across the room until it died in the evening and she would again survive it, lying in darkness. Her Silent Watcher stared upwards, saying nothing. She would like to kill herself, if she had the strength or freedom to do so, to take her rotting mind and kill it, to fuse her darkness with the world's and wait for the music, the wailing, the streaming bloody colours of Judgement Day. Tears made loud thumps and rustles in her ears.

*   *   *

Polly had been very naughty. You cannot eat flowers—they make you bilious—and Polly had nibbled the flowers embroidered on the cushions,

181

so she had been reprimanded and shut in her room until she could behave like a lady, and that ended the game. Polly sat on her shelf stiff-legged, reproved, staring into space. Abigail set off, leaving her there.

Her boots clobbered on the floorboards as she ran. Her mother greeted her with, 'Who is this trotting pony?'

'It's me,' Abigail said and fell against her mother's legs.

'Well, do try and make less noise,' she was told. 'And stand on your own feet, child.'

Abigail felt her mother's hand over her head, the fingers spread too tightly over her skull, and with ease Eliza pulled her upright. Abigail stood solitary, deprived of that merging contact. She stared up at her mother.

'Child, I am occupied at present.' A new patient was shortly to arrive whom she would have to receive, Matthew being away at the factory. And that was only her immediate concern. Eliza, while in her husband's study finding the admissions book, had seen a page of his calculations. If she had understood them correctly, then the investment was deep. It had put a sea beneath them with the establishment riding on it. It was a good thing her husband was who he was. She had reminded herself of that, but found that she kept needing to.

Abigail stretched up a hand. Eliza grasped it, rocked it from side to side and released it. 'Go and play,' she said and walked away.

With a painful bulk of anger and sadness inside her, Abigail watched her mother withdraw. She stood there panting until her mother was gone, then ran away again on her terrible loud boots.

One of Alfred Tennyson's significant deficiencies, Hannah had decided, was his lack of conversation. This was not unimportant. It had rendered matters practically impossible. Conversation was one of Hannah's only resources. With conversation she could engage and entangle and forge the strong sympathy of, well, possible lovers, and she had certainly tried that with Tennyson, but he'd been dull, unresponsive, dumb as a beast. There was that one occasion on which he'd done that extraordinary thing with his face and he'd been amiable. The rest of the time all her brilliance had elicited only faint glimmerings. Her attention was a light shone into murky water that had revealed gloomy inward depths, but she'd seen nothing more, nothing provocative of hope. Besides, it wasn't charitable to notice it, but he wasn't clean and he did smell. Of course poets made themselves sound exciting and wonderful in their poems; the reality was bound to be different. It was unfair, really, that other sorts of people were not written about so much.

Now, Charles Seymour was someone who engaged readily in conversation. He was social and open, a gentleman, and probably lonely, with his broken heart slowly healing. He was evidently an intelligent man, but he was courteous and to a greater extent available to others. He was not always away inside himself making poems for the journals to read and dislike.

Hannah was seated in her room making out a list of possible subjects for conversation when Abigail ran in and found her. Her page read:

Hunting—the excitement. Does he? Queen
Elizabeth hunting in this forest.
The young queen and Lord Melbourne.
Virtue and experience. Has he met her?
The best society being of like-minded people,
regardless of rank.
India.
The waning public taste for poetry.

She closed her journal as Abigail ran in and held
out her hands to her. Abigail charged between
them and bumped into her knees. 'Ooh,' Abigail
said, doing one of her impressions of the patients,
moaning and fidgeting and holding her hair.
'Don't do that,' Hannah instructed, taking hold
of her wrists. 'Now, tell me, little sister, what do
you like to talk about?'
'Farms,' Abigail replied.
'Indeed? Farms?'
Abigail nodded. 'Farms. Or presents.'
'Come here,' Hannah said, and fitted her hands
into Abigail's warm armpits and lifted her onto her
knee.

*   *   *

It was worse, worse even than the absence. Her
Silent Watcher stared out in desperation, but there
was nowhere to go.
It seemed her husband had returned, or someone
like him, stronger even and more determined. He
would stand and watch her relieve herself in her
chamber pot before he started.
Sometimes there were two of them.
Days grew light then dark against her window. It

184

was the dark that brought him. She prayed. She prayed with every waking thought, her whole being a shout that was not heard, brought no release. They had her in that room. At night, not every night, but unpredictably, they came.

*   *   *

Hannah had observed him for long enough now to know his habits, had watched through a narrow vivid strip in her drawn bedroom curtains. They were usefully regular and today she deployed herself to cross his path. She waited at her chosen place. The day was fine. Her hair would look well in the autumnal sunlight that lit branches and moss, formed soft gold pools between the trees. Nearby a rattling holly bush shone with berries. There was a distant sweet aroma from the charcoal burners: they must have opened a pile and were now scooping it into sacks. Beside the path, blackberries hung from long, straying loops of thorn. She picked one and put it in her mouth. It dissolved in a smear of flavour, sharp, thin, alert.

And then he was approaching, as planned, hat in hand, along the path. But what was she doing there? He must have seen her standing there doing nothing. How could she not have thought of this? But it was immediately obvious what to do. She started picking more berries, crushing them as she plucked with nervous, indelicate fingers. She had been looking at him when she saw him and he had most likely seen her. Now she was looking away as though she hadn't seen him. What would he think of that? And she had nothing to put the berries in, no receptacle, except her other hand. She laid

185

them, dented and leaking, in her left palm.

'Good day,' he called, waving his hat.

She turned, attempted but overemphasised and made unconvincing the appearance of having seen him for the first time. 'Mr Seymour, good day to you,' she answered and made a shallow curtsy.

'Picking blackberries?'

'Yes, I was walking and saw them and thought . . .'

'Do excuse me,' he said. She felt his fingertips on her skin as he took one from her hand and ate it. 'But you don't have anything to carry them in.'

'Yes, I do. I mean to say, I'll only gather a few.'

'Here.' He offered her his hat.

'But they'll stain.'

'The inside. And, anyway, what's a hat?'

Hannah, trying to respond to the question, found herself suddenly philosophically stumped, her mind full of abstract hat.

'Or, wait. Here,' he said, taking a handkerchief from his pocket and spreading it inside his hat.

'Oh, thank you.' She dropped her handful in.

'I like this path,' he said.

'Do you?'

'Hmm. It's one of the more attractive ways, don't you think? Can be dreary here. And I like to get away from Alfred.'

She panicked at the name. 'From whom?'

'My man, my valet. I can't have him looming behind me all day; it is tiresome. Careful. Stand aside.'

He spread his arms as though shooing geese, keeping her to the edge of the path. Hannah hadn't heard the pony approaching behind her. It passed: stocky, skewbald, with shaggy fetlocks, without a saddle, and with a young boy on its back.

The boy wore loose, laceless boots. He touched his hat. Charles Seymour did not acknowledge the gypsy's greeting. A few yards on the boy turned the pony from the path and began vanishing and appearing between the trees.

'Gypsy,' Charles Seymour said. His soft fair hair was beautifully lit by the sun. 'Good thing I was here.'

'Do you hunt?' Hannah asked.

'I do,' he said. 'Why do you ask?'

'Oh, I simply thought, well, it must be very thrilling, and perhaps you miss it.'

'Speaking truly, it is not the first thing that I am missing.'

Her heart thumped. Unable to think of anything else to say and unable to picture her list for a change of subject, a way out of the moment, she said, 'Sentimental attachments?'

He raised his eyebrows. 'Does your father tell you everything?'

'No, no, not at all. You mustn't think that. But, you see, you wouldn't be the first young gentleman of rank to be here for that reason, and clearly you aren't a lunatic.'

'I see. Perhaps it would be better if I were,' he said vaguely.

'Don't say that.' She was warming to her role as fearless interlocutor. Now she offered important advice. 'I think that the thing is to be definite and courageous, to be strong with yourself. If I may claim any experience.'

He widened his eyes. 'May you?' She said nothing, confused and reddening. 'I'm sorry,' he said. He hung his head and thought for a moment, then looked up, inhaling sharply. 'Would you like to pick any more?'

'Oh, yes.' Hannah leaned forward to do so. 'Will you remain here much longer?' she asked, facing away from him.

'I am to be kept here for a while yet. Her family believe me mad, but the fear, you see, is elopement.'

'I see. And would you?'

'Really you are an extraordinary girl—discussing such things alone with a gentleman. I suppose your situation is extraordinary. Talking to lunatics all day.'

'I suppose it is. It doesn't feel extraordinary. And I rarely talk to lunatics although, unless my . . . circumstances change, I will be expected to work with my mother soon enough.'

'Let's hope that doesn't happen.'

'Yes, let's.'

'But to answer your question, I suppose, now that you've asked it, it is . . . it is difficult to establish a household with nothing. She has nothing. I would be cut off. Do you think that ugly and prosaic? I think you do. Nevertheless . . . good day!'

'I beg your pardon?'

'Good day.'

Hannah turned to see another rider approaching. Thomas Rawnsley on a well-brushed bay. He lifted his hat.

'Good day to you.'

'Do you two,' Hannah stuttered, 'do you often collide?'

'I don't know about that,' Rawnsley answered, wearing an expression of humorous confusion.

'You have flowers,' Seymour said, patting the horse's neck with a rider's firm slaps.

'I do, I do,' Rawnsley answered, swivelling in his saddle to take them from the saddlebag.

'Roses,' Hannah said. 'At this time of year.'

'Yes. I had them from a friend's glasshouse. Here, why don't you take them?' He handed them down to Hannah. Yellow roses, with a cold, fresh fragrance, wrapped in paper.

Hannah held them, was silent. Thomas Rawnsley saw that they pained her. He eased her mind. 'I thought you might give them to your mother. I imagine they might brighten a corner. Well, I won't keep you. Good day.'

When Hannah returned home, a note was waiting for her. 'Dear Hannah, the roses were for you. I hope it does not distress you to learn this. Perhaps you will look on them and think of me. Respectfully, Thomas Rawnsley.'

*   *   *

Lord Byron was awoken. The bolt of his chamber door was lifted, slapped across. The door swung open. He wiped his mouth and sat up, then scratched himself thoroughly through warm, soiled clothes.

Lights bounced in the corridor outside, the servants' swinging lanterns as they opened other doors.

In truth, Byron did not greatly enjoy these night-time revels. The tumult of high spirits around him sharpened the sensation of his own solitude, his lofty and painful isolation. But he liked to step out if his door was opened, not only because if he did not do so of his own free will, a servant would return and grab him and damn near throw him down the stairs, but because he liked to sidle round and test whether the front door had also been unlocked. If it had been, he could slip out finally, finally escape into the night.

People slouched past his door to the stairs, moaning and shuffling. He stepped out to join them. Their voices were quieter than those of the people still in their cells yelling to be let out. At the bottom of the stairs, bottles were being opened. A fiddle, unwrapped from a blanket, was put in the hands of one who knew how to play. Lord Byron, who played himself, felt slighted, but recalled that he kept this talent a secret here, that he preferred to play among gypsies and free men.

He stepped through the throng, carefully out towards the front door. Locked. He could smell the cold world outside and pressed himself flat against the wood. A sliver of air breathed through a crack onto his eyeball. He blinked.

'Away from there.' A heavy slap on his back. 'Drink, instead, old fellow me lad. Let's all be jolly, eh. Who's your money on tonight?' He accepted the bottle. The servant's friendly hand gripped the meat of his neck as he swallowed a long flame of liquor. 'There's a lad.' He took another swig.

'Flash company,' said Lord Byron.

'What's that?' The servant raised his voice over the shrieks and barks and pleadings of the other revellers.

'Flash company. I used to gad about with in London. Glory days. My reputation then at its zenith.'

'That so?'

'You give your all. You sing and sing. You write your heart wide open and in the end the crowd turns, will insult you, will tread on that heart as they rush to a new amusement.'

The servant didn't answer this. His head was turned away as he shouted, 'Lay in!'

Byron wiped his eyes and watched the ruction of bodies. Servants pulled one man from another to restart the bout. Confused, seated heavily on his arse, piebald with blood on his face, the man was helped up onto his feet. A servant whispered into his ear as the man wiped the greasy blood onto his fingers and licked them. Whatever that servant said had a clear inspiriting effect. The fighter's face fell open with grief and rage and he ran at his opponent. The fiddle played, a thin lonely thread curving among the claps and cheers and sobbing and shrieks. Two men were being unnatural in the shadows; he could see their stiff thrusts. Another suddenly screamed loudly enough to get everybody's attention and fell into a fit, his rigid arms circling slowly in front of him, his eyes white, breath snoring and seething in his throat. An attendant stood over him and poured drink, or tried to, into his mouth.

John Byron looked away. This was not the proper thing, not the sport he loved. As the men tumbled he heard a head knock against the floorboards, clear and sharp as a stonemason's hammer, and there was laughter. A full moon, he noticed, looking away. He saw that one of the small, high windows was crammed with its cold white. A doctor acquaintance of his had once told him that a full moon vexed the mad. They certainly seemed vexed. He passed the bottle to another. Drink was not having its enlivening effect this evening. He wasn't feeling freer or warmer.

191

Instead he was simply loosed into his melancholy, drifting down and down.

In the commotion it seemed possible that he could slip away, back to his room to rest and perhaps even regain himself with a little versing. Slowly, he abstracted himself from the bellowing crowd and crept back upstairs.

He passed a door that still juddered with the impacts of one angry to be pent inside, past one of soft moaning, and one that was ajar and that he knew immediately was wrong. He wouldn't have been able to say how he knew, but those stifled voices . . . he just knew. Gently, with his fingertips, he pushed the door further open. Legs along the floor, a man shoving, another man standing, his face in shadow, a lamp by her head, and as she sensed him in the doorway, her head rolling slowly towards him. Mary! No, no, not Mary. Her eyes were dark and open and still. They fluttered slightly in the breath of the shoving man, but their gaze was so deep Byron felt himself almost falling towards them, as though the floor sloped down into a pit and she was at the bottom staring up. From deep inside herself she seemed to watch him and beg for his help. Below those eyes her mouth was moving. Go to . . . no. God is . . . something. God is . . . something. She looked like Mary, didn't she, a bit? Byron felt his face crumpling as he started to cry.

Stockdale noticed her staring and turned, staring back over his shoulder. 'You,' he said.

'No, no, no,' Byron said. 'I never. Just let me go back to my room.'

Stockdale was up and out of her, walking towards John, not bothering to cover himself, distended, wet and raw. Behind him, the woman held her part with one hand, crossed herself with the other. The shadowed man knelt down on her chest.

'Let me go back to my room.'

'How mad are you?' Stockdale asked, finally tucking himself away. 'What do you know?'

'I know when I smell sulphur. I know when people have forgotten shame.'

'So mad, then.'

'I know when crimes are committed. I, Lord Byron, have spoken against slavery and abuse.'

'You didn't see anything and you won't remember anything.' Stockdale drew back his right hand and threw his fist into John's face. He saw the attendant's knuckles suddenly huge, big as the palings of a fence with creases of shadow between them as his eye was struck, a vivid visual arrest he was still pondering when the second shadowy blow swum like a pike towards him and knocked him out cold.

*   *   *

Alone together in Hannah's room, their conversation veered between the worldly, ladylike and implicit, and the girlish, rapid and amazed. Hannah had decided for the first time not to tell Annabella everything, it being perhaps better for her not to meet Charles Seymour. His was the name Hannah did not say. Her silences and elisions were full of him. Rawnsley she would perhaps talk about. They could disparage him together.

Annabella used Hannah's brushes on her own thick, dark hair. They made a scuffing, electrical

193

sound. Annabella looked very maidenly or mermaidly with her untied hair draped over her shoulders, although her facial expression, vacant with concentration, looked to Hannah like a small girl's or an animal's.

Hannah found that she could talk about Alfred Tennyson. The poet's name, when she said it, was cool and solid in her mouth. Very recently it had dragged after it a sensation of panicking flight.

'Oh, yes. I saw him the other day,' Annabella said. Tilting her head and brushing her hair into a gathering hand, she stared up at the ceiling.

'Did you?' This did make Hannah start, that she did not know about this.

'Yes, I did. Wrapped in his cloak, out in the cold fog,' she said in her recitation voice. 'Amid the spectral trees.'

There was that tone of light scorn, of satire, and it displeased Hannah. She could dislike Tennyson, but not easily find him comical yet. And it suggested that Alfred Tennyson would not have been considered good enough for Annabella. She was a nymph or dryad to him. She was a nymph or dryad to everyone. She would wait and make a choice.

'Did you speak to him?'

'I said "Good day" and he answered "Good day".' She had imitated his Lincolnshire accent unsuccessfully and tried again. ' "Good day," and raised his hat off all that tangled hair and walked on.'

Hannah was suddenly, surprisingly, angered by this. She didn't like the thought of these people out there moving independently, meeting and having conversations she would never hear, not thinking of her. It killed her, made a ghost of her. And even if she had given up on Tennyson, she did not like Annabella's contemptuous tone. It was too typical of the person that she knew lurked behind that beauty.

'Perhaps he had no desire to talk to you because he was thinking more interesting thoughts.'

'What's that?'

'Simply because you are so beautiful, Anna, doesn't mean the whole world has to fall down and worship you.'

'What?' Annabella asked again dumbly, her face innocent and stricken. She blushed in that ridiculously pretty way she had—two thumbprints of rouge above her dimples—not the painful red stain Hannah could feel spreading up from her neck.

'I know that you can have anyone you want to have. You know you're beautiful. You don't have to try and pretend: oh, no, I'm just a plain simple comfortable girl.'

'Why are you saying this?'

'Because.'

Hannah didn't know quite why. She was much angrier than she could have anticipated. Annabella's beauty was not fair; it pulled the world towards her, drew in her future without effort, and Hannah was sick of pretending it wasn't there. It was as though she were conniving in her own betrayal, knowing that Annabella would safely, lightly, contemptuously surpass her at any moment she chose. They could not be real friends, Hannah decided at that moment, because they were not equals.

Nor was she given time, in fact, to change her

mind. There was a knock at the door. It was opened by Fulton. He bowed with flirtatious gallantry to Annabella and said with a smirk to his sister, 'You have a visitor.'

'He did call me nymph,' Annabella called after her as she left. 'Did your poet call you that?'

At the bottom of the stairs, Hannah found Thomas Rawnsley. Waiting outside were two horses. Hannah was invited to ride the good-natured grey. He stood behind her as she climbed onto a new two-pommelled saddle, the leather glossy and uncracked and smelling of the workshop.

'So where shall we ride then?'

He looked startled, almost hurt. 'Nowhere in particular. Just through the woods. The air and so forth. I thought you might enjoy it.'

This had become a very agitating day. After so much panting and wishing and waiting and sighing, after so much nothing at all, life was finally happening, but not at all as she'd imagined. Firstly, an argument with Annabella and now, to escape from her, this ride. For much of the time she thought of the argument with clenchings of alternating regret and determination. Thomas Rawnsley rarely interrupted her. Although his intent was now overt, unquestionable, he did not seem to be making an effort to entertain her into an affection for him. He was not charming or expansive. He was not free and light like Charles Seymour. Nor did he have the profound, productive quiet of Tennyson. He was literal, direct and uncomfortable. His courtship (which this was, it seemed) was sullen and congested. Apparently it pained him. It was serious. Unlike the poet or aristocrat, he worked. It had made him rich, but the wealth sat on him like a garland, brittle and separate. Really, he was the work. His name suggested it. Rawnsley. Rawnsley. Hannah didn't like that dragging long first vowel. What did it remind her of? Tawny. Brawny. Yes, brawn: the meat. Still, his clothes were beautiful, his possessions—his gloves, these horses—pristine. It was interesting, at least theoretically, to think that his wife would be similarly outfitted, sealed inside that wealth, sleek and secure and widely acknowledged.

The forest was darkening. Winter was not far off. The black fallen leaves, plastered down by heavy rain, were silvered here and there with frost. The tree trunks were wet. They passed the hooked, blustery shine of a holly. Good snail weather. Their reins creaked. The bits clicked in the horses' mouths as they breathed large clouds. Hannah felt sorry for Rawnsley when his horse manured. He seemed visibly embarrassed by it, staring, stiff-necked, into the distance, as though he himself had done it.

The quiet was very calming. It was pleasant not talking. After a while Rawnsley said, 'Would you allow me to show you something?'

'Of course. I'm intrigued,' she said politely.

They plodded on along soft paths until Thomas Rawnsley halted them. He turned with bright eyes and a finger pressed to his lips. Hannah's day continued to work its elaborate stage machinery with another peculiar revelation. What Rawnsley then pointed to through the trees, and clearly in some way delighted him, was a gypsy camp. A fizzing, wet fire, dogs and horses and caravans, that unbounded, illicit life she had been taught always to avoid. They would steal from her. They might even steal her. The sight of them, at a safe distance and while she was protected beside Rawnsley, filled her with a lovely, crisp-edged fear and pleasure. She smiled at Rawnsley, who smiled back. They sat on their shifting horses and stared a moment longer, then rode quietly away.

Winter

The bishop's chair was a church in itself: high-backed, winged, with projecting arms bearing candlesticks to afford illumination for reading and a shelf in its side for books. A small table with a lamp and gleaming spectacles stood close to this edifice.

Matthew Allen's chair, set across the patterned rug at the other end of the fireplace's breadth of stone, was less grand, but nevertheless deep and supportive. Not that he was getting the benefit of it. His body was still rocking with the ghostly motions of his long journey, the train and jouncing carriage, and he was not at all relaxed. He gripped the armrests and smiled.

The bishop had a kind and dignified face, of the grand and passionless type of piety. His pale eyes were set in large orbits, his lips were full and set back beneath a long, arched, nacreous nose. His sideburns were a rich white trim. He looked well fed, well kempt. The cracked brown portraits of previous bishops Matthew Allen had passed on his way through the palace had included many harder, more austere faces set on stiff ruffs.

The palace inspired violent emotions in Dr Allen. He felt goaded by the fierce, thin ghost of his father, could hear his voice pouring scorn on the complacent wealth of the established church, its spiritual torpitude. The relentless Sandemanian would not have admired the large cross of chased silver on the mantel shelf, or the painting of Christ that was in the line of Matthew's gaze: a varnished, dark Italianate Jesus, head bowed, with strong, sensual shoulders and the doleful dark eyes of a

201

deer. His father's Christ had been like himself: lean, definite, endlessly imparting the truth, presumably with the same spittle-flecked lips and reddened throat. He was a narrow lever inserted into ancient Palestine to turn the whole world over. Nothing here was turning over. Everything was still, solid, polished and would outlast the flesh of the two men now seated there.

The palace reminded him also of university and provoked both a passionate recoil and a desire to stay there, to be welcomed. His debts had forced him from university. After that had come a shop and evening classes. If the bishop agreed to more time for the manufacture, Allen would love the place and belong there. If not, he would know he had been right about it all along.

When a servant entered bearing tea, Allen bent forward in his seat. The servant was instructed to pour immediately because, unfortunately, the bishop hadn't much time. Allen watched as the bishop's tea was poured through a strainer into the porcelain cup and a short ribbon of milk was added. He accepted the same service for himself, the calming, intimate, impersonal ritual, like a visit to the barber, and felt afterwards cleaner, better equipped to continue the conversation.

'So, I am sure you understand, your grace, that these technical difficulties represent an entirely surmountable obstacle. I am perfectly confident that I will be able to inform you that I can supply the carvings required in one or two months.'

The bishop, blowing on his tea, answered, 'That is good news. I have seven churches in my diocese, doctor, that as you know are awaiting their fittings. In this part of the North Country, with the new industrial parishes, we have great need of them.'

'And they will be supplied.'

'In one month?'

'In one or two months.'

'In one month?'

'Assuming that the technical difficulties are . . . the required refitting has occurred . . . the part of the machine that needs replacement has been replaced, replaced, then yes, in one month.'

'I'm afraid I heard rather a lot of dependent clauses in that sentence.'

Matthew Allen moved his teacup from hand to hand. 'I cannot guarantee that everything will be ready in one month.'

'That is disappointing. I had hoped to be able to rely on you and conclude our work together, but given this delay I am sure you will understand if we approach an established workshop.'

'I can fulfil the order.'

'Not in time. You have just said that you cannot. I'm sorry, I have no wish to argue with you. Can you guarantee delivery in one month's time?' The bishop regarded Allen with raised eyebrows, the fine ridge of his nose lengthened and shining.

'No.'

'Very well, then. That is a disappointment. Now, if you will excuse me.'

'But we have a contract.'

'I hope you are not intending to haggle with me like an Israelite merchant. I believe we had an agreement and not a contract, as a matter of fact. I am very sorry that this journey has been wasted for you, and I do wish you success in the future for your enterprise. As you have explained it to me, I cannot see how you would not succeed. Now, if you would excuse me.'

The bishop rose from his elaborate chair and Matthew Allen stood also, as was required. Holding his teacup in both hands, with nowhere to set it down, he bowed to the bishop as he left the room.

*   *   *

With her father still away, her mother gone with all the servants to deal with the laundry in Fairmead House, it was Hannah herself who opened the door to Thomas Rawnsley. He looked startled at the sight of her, flinched a little more upright, but cleverly melded the motion with the sweeping off of his hat.

'Hannah,' he said. 'These . . .'

'Yes?'

'These roses . . .'

'Yes?'

'Well, they're for you, aren't they?'

*   *   *

In his room at the inn, Matthew Allen stood in his shirtsleeves by the window, looking down at the rain spluttering on the cobbles of the courtyard, the maids hurrying from door to door. The dark-beamed ceiling was low over his head. Brandy had softened him. He stood in this box and thought. The money coming in and the money going out. The demands for dividends and the orders placed. They were colliding. He was being crushed between two columns of a ledger. The hope and air were being crushed out of him. He drank more and decided that, being realistic, the whole thing was over and they would lose everything. People did not know what it meant to lose everything, but he did. He'd been in a debtors' prison, between dark walls, denied the liberty to act, made an infant, an inmate, between dark walls. To have to beg money to start over—who would dream of lending him money now, after this? There was no light. He was crushed.

He wondered if it was possible to kill yourself by drinking a whole bottle of brandy in one go and decided to try. He raised the bottle to his lips, tipped his head back and drank, watching big bubbles flip up to its base. He shouted as he thumped the bottle down on the table and wiped his eyes, burping a sickening hot vapour. 'Not enough,' he moaned. It would take three or four. 'Not enough. Or. Or.' He stumbled over to the mirror, catching the wall with an outstretched hand, and stared at his face, his wet, scorched lips and hard, hostile eyes. 'No,' he said. 'No, no, no, no, no. Not yet. Not yet. Can be done. Bloody. By me. Don't die, old fellow. Here's what . . . what'll . . .' He walked erect, then fell forwards onto his bed, reaching for his portfolio, for pen and paper, to write to Tennyson.

He lay there, with the room circling slowly around him and phrases forming in his mind. 'Immense,' he said out loud. 'Immense.' He sat up and wrote.

. . . We shall have an immense business. All is hope, fear is gone and I feel happy. We are all safe. If you knew the proportion of anxiety that I have gone through and the feeling of

205

relief that overwhelms me and often makes my head swell to bursting with gratitude and relieved only by tears scampering over my eyelids, you would see the depth and sincerity of the heart of the man who calls himself your friend, and who trusts in God, that he will be able to give the lie to all those who were suspicious, but far be it from me to boast, far be it from me to say a word against anyone.

Orders are flowing in from all the great ones. The Bishop of Chester has added four chairs to his order. Never was anything more promising. All things are a lie and all things are false if this fails. The world and human nature might be changed, but it is not so and will not be so.

*   *   *

Tennyson sat by his fire sinking into the grief that will make him famous. When the grief was total and full of questions, full of words, was a world itself, when he'd written it, when the young queen's young husband had died and she'd let it be known that Tennyson's poem was the great assuagement and elaboration of her own grief, then Tennyson will be laureate, will be rich, will be one of the great men of the age, known and praised throughout the Empire. He will meet the queen at her residence on the Isle of Wight. Before he goes, his wife will brush the sand from his boots, brush his clothes and his hair. Then he will find himself standing by a fireplace, hearing a door open and turning to see his queen enter, or half-see it. His eyes will be even weaker and they will fill instantly with tears of admiration and joy. 'I am like your lonely Mariana now,' the queen will say to him, and Tennyson, not knowing what to say, will blurt, 'What a king Prince Albert would have made.' He will fear having spoken grossly, but she will nod and agree. Tennyson will feel an understanding there between them in that room, a mingling of lonely, frail, slow spirits like the merging of clouds. But at present it was simply grief, coarse and brackish and tiring. It did not feel like success. It did not feel like an illuminated future. It felt like loneliness and a slowly throbbing rage and confusion.

He had not lit the lamps and in the gloom of the early winter evening his long fingernails shone with the fire's red, a warmer red than the sunset's crimson, which, if he turned, he could see broken by tree shapes, blotting the surface of the frozen pond. Gules, he thought, all gules. That heraldic blood-red. That was something. His mind moved towards it. On the forest floor the shattered lances. The shattered lances lay on the hoof-churned mud. An ancient English wood where knights had ridden, where Queen Elizabeth hunted, where Shakespeare rode, according to the doctor's daughter, to play out his Dream in an aristocrat's hall. Twilight in that place, soft decay, the soft sun finding some scattered remains. There was something there: an English epic, a return of Arthur. An English Homer. Blood and battle and manliness and the machine of fate. He could hear its music, ringing, metallic and deep with inward echoings. His mind approached it, felt along the flank of this thing. It would be worth the attempt, if he ever had the strength. The logs hissed and smoked. The forest outside was again dreary, darkening, factual. There was nobody there.

His friends were elsewhere. Septimus was in the doctor's madhouse. His brother Edward was in another. His father was dead. Arthur Hallam, his friend, was dead and had taken out of the world with him energy, air, life. The greatest mind Alfred had known: widely commanding, clear and quick, inventive, adult, poetic. Arthur had loved Alfred's poetry, had defended it in print, he had loved Alfred and he was dead. He would have married Alfred's sister, would have become the best element in his family, but he had died and left Alfred alone.

Images of Arthur came and went, but no words came. Words would come, he might have known that, but presently they did not. He was dumb and alone. He lacked the energy even to read other people's words or get up from his chair. He stared at the fire. He was alone.

*   *   *

Dr Matthew Allen sat at his desk with a cup of coffee and a pen in his hand. He had a new ledger open in front of him and carefully entered invented numbers that would appease his investors. At moments he looked down at his solidified lies and it made his scalp tighten, but he reminded himself of their honourable and logical purpose. When dealing with the mad a virtuous dishonesty is sometimes required. So with his investors: he would mislead them to ultimate rewards. His heart beat light and fast with the pleasure of his own cleverness.

Still, the need for actual money remained. Fortunately he had thought of somebody to ask before the last resort of writing to his brother Oswald. Humming to himself, he got up, smoothed down his beard and set off for their room.

He knocked softly and heard nothing. He opened the door and entered. Septimus, fully clothed, lay curled on his bed, his knees up to his chest, his hands hugging his knees. 'Good morning,' said Matthew. 'Just the man.'

*   *   *

Lord Byron awoke with a fearsome headache, in soiled garments. He knew he only had himself to blame, but without such dissipations how could he disperse his animal spirits and find rest? The pages he had written! There had been weeks of thousands of lines, his hand scurrying across the page hurrying to set them down, his lip fluttering, his head a butter churn of beating poetry. His family would be snoring before he fell asleep and he would awaken when the stars were just beginning to sink into dawn's flood of light and the first people were trudging out to the fields, his lips already moving with lines he had to set down. Poems had formed in his dreams, had become louder and clearer until they had formed a solid bridge into wakefulness. They would force him awake to serve them. Sometimes he would creep out of bed into his corner chair, find an unused scrap of paper and start scratching them down before he realised that he'd written them already. Weeks of this frenzy. No wonder John Barleycorn was called upon to loosen the grip of words, to set him back on his arse and out of the violent machine of poetry.

But it had been better with his friends, a companionable riot through London's streets. They would hate to see him now, alone in his room, hungry, abandoned, in a soiled shirt and excremental undergarments. And in flashes, with sudden clenches of shame, images of the past night's debauch recurred to him. Had there really been again such ungentlemanly fighting? And fornication? He remembered shrieks and heard more of them from other parts of his house.

His servant opened the door. 'Time for your exercise,' he said.

Byron looked at him, remembering. 'Yes,' he said quietly and stood, still staring at the man. His servant's face changed as he stared, or rather, stayed the same, became the same. Around that face the air seemed to be splitting, dragging back. It was excruciating to watch. The face pushed into a new element, as though through water, until it was absolutely there, in the room with him. Finally, Byron recognised the man.

'I know who you are.'

'I know who you are.'

'I know what you do.'

'Do you, now?'

Behind the man, his double, himself, face glossy with sweat, buttoning his trousers, merging into the back of himself.

'You're Stockdale.'

'And who are you?'

'Lord Byron. I know what you do.'

'You don't know anything, your lordship.'

'You did it again last night.'

'Your lordship is mistaken. You've been locked up these past three days.'

'Three nights ago, then. You violated . . .'

'Come, come. Don't be foolish.'

'Give me my liberty and I won't tell.'

'Your freedom is for the doctor to decide. And anyway, who would believe you?'

'The doctor.'

'Which doctor?'

'Dr Allen. He is a friend of mine.'

'Put you in here, though, didn't he? Your friend. You see, you are mad.'

'I'm not.'

'Who are you?'

'Don't think . . .' Byron held his head.

'Who are you?'

'Ow.'

He had to, he had to pull himself back inside himself. Stockdale had hold of his shirt, was shaking him. He clenched his teeth. Inside his skull, a crushing, a drowning. He forced himself further. He had to. It was an exchange of pains and he had to accept the greater. Stockdale shook him. John felt his flesh come off in the attendant's hands leaving his bones bare, like a dead beast's bones tacky with remnant flesh where the wind and sun had burned. Only his head remained the same. He heard the knocking of dogs' jaws busy around his entrails that hung and fell into a pit. Stockdale dropped him. When he landed he saw himself briefly on a road, fleshless, exposed, a dead rabbit. He heard the clatter of carts and voices. Alone. The road stretched for miles in each direction. The wind softly blew on him. He'd woken up so far from home. He knew who he was.

'I'm John,' he said.

'Who are you?'

'I'm John Clare. I'm John. I'm a celebrated poet. When the doctor makes his rounds I will tell him what you did, unless you tell him to release me, that I am better.'

'You don't know who you are. Shakespeare, is it? Nelson? Who are you?'

'You know who I am. You will tell him to release me. And her. You let her go, too.'

'Who?'

'Mary?'

'Mary? There is no Mary here.'

'Not Mary. You know who. You know.'

*   *   *

Winter was ending in a long ceremony of rain, rain with hardly any wind beyond the drifting cold breath of its downrush. Vertical and loud, it flattened the grass and shone in all the trees.

Dr Allen stepped out into it, raising his umbrella. He was late and hungry. He hadn't eaten that morning. He hadn't dared, what with the pain in his stomach and the lightest of meals causing violent expulsions. He lacked regularity. He lacked sleep. He lacked money.

A figure on the path, also under an umbrella.

'Dr Allen,' he shouted over the noise of the rain.

'Yes.' Dr Allen squinted at him, holding his collar.

'You are Dr Allen?'

'Yes.'

'Then you're the devil I want,' he shouted.

'I beg your pardon?'

'Yes, you will.'

'I'm sorry, are you a patient?'

'How dare you!'

The rain drummed on the man's umbrella, formed a falling fringe of drops in front of his glaring red face. Dr Allen suffered a sudden lurch of panic: the man was a creditor.

'I'm terribly sorry,' he said. 'Please, come inside. We can't talk like this out in the rain. I can hardly hear you.'

'It takes you this long to invite me inside. Lead on, doctor, lead on.'

Whoever he was followed Matthew Allen into the vestibule, furled his umbrella and speared it into the stand.

'I knew,' he began, 'that you ran a lax establishment, but I thought that at least you would know who was and was not a patient of yours.'

'Many apologies for the confusion. Sincerely. If you would please follow me to my study. There we can talk.'

Allen set off swiftly towards his study, wanting to conceal whatever would follow, to bottle it. He opened the door and the man strode past him—past, frighteningly, the two sets of accounts laid side by side, but at which he did not glance.

'What's that?' the man asked, pointing.

'Oh, that. That's an orrery. It's the planets.'

'Yes, yes. I know what it is. I'd forgotten the name.'

'If I may explain,' Allen said. 'There have been difficulties, as I've acknowledged, of a mechanical nature, but as I have tried to make clear, the machine is now functioning perfectly . . .'

213

'Machine? What are you talking about?'

'The Pyroglyph. Excuse me, sir, you are . . .'

'Excuse me, "your lordship" is the appropriate form of address for a viscount.'

'For a viscount?'

'Indeed. A viscount.'

Allen began to wonder if this were not, in fact, a patient, one of the new ones his wife had been dealing with. 'I beg your pardon . . .'

'So you will when I've finished with you. Do you really have no idea what is going on?'

'I'm sorry. I'm a little unwell. The machine, the manufacture, the accounts take up a great deal of energy.'

'Will you stop talking about your bloody machine.'

'I'm sorry, I don't understand.'

'Don't understand. Don't know. My son is a patient, so to speak. Charles Seymour. His name is familiar, at least?'

'Oh. Oh. Of course. I do beg your pardon, your lordship.'

'As predicted. Would you summon him for me?'

'If you so wish.'

'I do wish it. I wish it very much, very much. But it can't be done. You can't do it. And once again I am appalled that you don't know that you can't. You can't because he is not here. He has done exactly what I have been paying you to avoid. He has run off with that atrocious little whore.'

Spring

Morning. The door open. Stepping out into light, into the world carefully, one step at a time so as not to fall. Inhaling her small requirement of the boundless air. Leaves on the trees, green growth in the vegetable garden where the people quietly worked. Nothing came at her, nothing attacked. There were flowers and clouds. The day was gentle.

Forgiveness. This was what forgiveness felt like—given back to the world, freed into it, whole and restored. Without words her being resonated thanks as she stood there, closing her eyes slowly in the breeze and opening them again to see the Creation, the play of the infant Christ's spirit in the subtle movement of life around her.

She saw the doctor's youngest child and called out to her. The child started, clutched its hands together. Perhaps she had frightened her during her task, after the angel, when she had been required to be fierce and incessant. She called again and smiled and the child approached her.

'Good day, Abigail. How are you?'

'Good day.'

The child shifted as it stood, wriggling, lifting its hands to its head, looking around. Margaret felt she could almost see its large, clear soul, too big for the compact body.

'It is lovely to see you.'

'Are you better?'

'The Lord protects, Abigail. The Lord protects. You can tell your father I forgive him. The Lord's compassion,' she laughed, raising both hands, 'is astounding.'

217

'Don't cry.'

'I'm not crying. Am I? I won't.'

'Good.' Abigail reached up and held her thin hand with her small, warm hand. 'Will you do more sewing now?'

* * *

Matthew Allen struggled to detach her grip from his arm, but as he pulled she twisted her grip into his sleeve. It was the thundery weather that made them worse, the noise, the wind buffeting the windows and wrenching through the woods, all the trees flaring upright in weird light. She asked him, 'Is it true? You won't turn me out, will you?'

'No. Not at all.'

'Will you?'

There were tears in her eyes. He prised at her fingers. He felt another hand on him, on his shoulder, pulling. These hands he wrestled with, in his fatigue: he felt as though they might pull him open finally, spill him like a suitcase full of clothes. He shook himself like an animal and turned. It was John.

'What is it?'

'I must talk with you.'

'Must you? Now?'

'Yes.'

'Let go of me, then.'

'You won't turn me out?' she repeated.

'No, we will not,' Matthew almost shouted, removing her hand by the wrist. 'Come to my study,' he said to John. 'I need, I . . . Let's just go.' He wiped his forehead with the back of his hand.

John walked behind the doctor and stared at the

218

back of his neck, the way it emerged, delicate and narrow, from the stiff ring of his collar. The furrow down the middle of it. The sparks of fair hair. The resistance in it, the effort of will.

Matthew Allen unlocked the door and ushered John into a private red gloom of papers and piled books. John watched as he opened the curtains.

The doctor sat heavily on a chair. 'So, what is it?' He rubbed his forehead with his fingertips and checked them for sweat, then wiped them on his trousers.

'It is my want of freedom,' John began, standing stout and justified in the middle of the rug. 'I must . . . you must . . . I must again be allowed beyond the confines of this place.'

'John, you understand . . .'

'Lord Radstock to you.'

'What?'

John saw the doctor checked in his response, looking weary and helpless, and felt his advantage.

'Well, there we are,' the doctor muttered. 'There we are.'

'Where are we? I'm here, stifled here. I need liberty. I demand liberty.'

'Do not shout. There's no need.'

'There is need. Look here, I had been intending not to tell you this, you little bottle imp, but if it comes to it, so be it. There are things happening here, violations . . .'

'I said there's no need to shout.' Matthew Allen surged to his feet. 'There is . . .' He started coughing and couldn't stop. John waited impatiently, but the fit took hold. The doctor's eyes thickened in their sockets, spit flew onto his purpling lips. He held up a hand to indicate that it

219

would pass. Eventually, in a few sputtering jerks, it relented. Allen moaned, breathed in carefully.

'You are unwell.'

Allen laughed. 'I fear you may be correct.' To himself, his voice sounded faint. Something had shifted inside his ears.

'And tired.'

'Oh, yes. And tired.'

'Then rest. Lie down. Lie down on your sofa.'

'Yes, yes, I will.'

Matthew accepted. Why not? Everyone pulling at him, requiring his decisions. Let them decide for a change. John stood over him as he subsided groaning down onto the cushions. John then took the blanket draped over the sofa's back rest and spread it as a coverlet over the doctor. Matthew Allen watched the broken poet's comfortable fat face as he tucked the blanket under his side so that he was snugly wrapped, and remembered that the poor man was a father like himself. He had tended fevered children with presumably that same look of abstract, practical care in his eyes. It made the doctor helpless for a moment, wanting to weep. John's short, dirty hands completed their task and he stood upright again.

'Thank you,' he said. He lay, exhausted and incapable of his own life, lying beneath it without the energy to continue. 'Thank you.'

'So, about my freedom.'

*　　　*　　　*

John turned his face towards the sun, the light split into beams by the branches. One of them, the size of an infant's vague kiss, played warmly on the corner of his eye and forehead. He squinted along it like a carpenter seeing if a plank was true. Soft with motes and pollen. A pair of circling transparent wings.

He walked over crackling dry twigs the storms had ripped out. Between oaks, occasional bluebells shivered together. Overhead, the weep of birds. The touch of the world. Glad of it. Yearning across it, for home. All the world was road until he was home.

At Buckhurst Hill church he emerged from the woods. The church with a face and aspect, there like a person, like a house. He walked through the stone gatehouse into its orderly garden of graves, the thickened silence where the dead lay. The yew with its dark, slow needles spread a decent gloom.

Inside the church he found the customary dry echoes, dark pews, figures frozen in the wildflower-coloured windows, and a woman sitting alone. He passed her as he walked up the aisle to cross himself before the altar. Mary! No, not Mary, another of the patients, that woman he had . . . saved from Stockdale. She was staring up at the cross and smiling with tears on her face. She did not glance at him. He had done that. He had saved her. A rising wind hummed against the glass and its frozen saints. He crept outside.

In the churchyard was a boy, resting apparently, dressed like a ploughboy in a smock. He looked about nine years old and neither smiled nor made a greeting. He looked as serious and tired as any working man and resembled, John realised, one of his own sons at that age: the same stout build, the same heavy, clean flesh of the face and eyelashes long against his cheek.

'I haven't a halfpenny,' John said and the boy met his eye finally, but did not reply. The breeze lifted the long hair from his forehead and he narrowed his eyes and that gave the effect of an answer. 'I would give you one otherwise.'

The boy looked at him, eventually raised a hand to thank John for the thought, then folded his arms.

John rambled back into the woods, the musky spring odour and wheeling light. He saw a tree lying on its side, barkless, stripped white, ghost-glimmering through the others. Strange for it to have been felled at this time of year, with the sap rising, making the trees strong and wilful and difficult. Perhaps it was diseased. And every shred of bark taken for the tanning trade. He pitied it, felt suddenly that he was it, lying there undefended, its grain tightening in the breeze. He hurried on.

They had moved. It took him some time to find them. When he did he was thirsty and tired. There were fewer of them, fewer horses, only two vardas. But the crone, Judith, was still there by the yog, staring into it, her face a mask painted with its light. She flinched at his approach; raising a shoulder, she made to get up. 'No,' he said. 'Judith, it's me.'

She squinted at him and relaxed with recognition. 'You've come among us again, John Clare. Sit. Are you well?'

'I am,' he said. But he wasn't. The day's warmth faded out of him suddenly. Each day different. Each day perishing. His life at an end.

*   *   *

222

Cliffs of stained brick on either side as the train rambled out through the slums. Filth in the gutters, running children, worn laundry restless in the wind, wretched lives packed behind windows. The world was in poor repair. Dr Allen knew that there was much he could do, if given the chance, if only he were listened to, looked up to and asked. But he wasn't. People would stop asking him anything when he was bankrupt, the asylum sold, rotting in gaol.

Beyond the city came the relief of countryside, standing cattle and wet lanes and carts and clouds. Usually, Matthew enjoyed travelling by train, travelling triumphantly at speed across a superseded world, the frightened labourers in the fields staring back at him, but he hadn't that ease today as he travelled towards Oswald and humiliation.

If Oswald did grant him a loan, then surely all would be well. The machine was now, more or less, working as it should. It had been a delay only; his inspiration, his enterprise was sound. More than that, it was brilliant. He knew he was brilliant. And his brother knew it too.

He looked at the wooden fittings of the carriage's interior. How were those contracts secured? Who was a wealthy man because of them? He should approach the rail companies himself. Just think of it: ticket offices, waiting rooms, lavatories—the railways teemed with places his wood carving could adorn. Oswald should be told that. Oswald was a fool. He too could be wealthy if only he could bring himself to admit his younger brother's brilliance.

'If you wouldn't mind. Your leg.'

A lady in the carriage, reading trash, had found the fidgeting of Dr Allen's leg irksome.

'I do beg your pardon.' He would have liked to treat her to a few days in the dark room, an ice bath, a clyster. Bloody hussy!

He would arrive at his brother's shop unannounced, just as his brother had arrived at High Beach. This avoided being told by letter in advance that the journey was useless and accorded Matthew the advantage of a personal appeal.

By the time the train had stumbled into York, Matthew was tired, his mood had so quickly and so violently varied from the exultant to the enraged. And the sight of York made him feel sick, a town in which he had not distinguished himself, had made no reputation, had been imprisoned, and where people might remember him.

He smoothed his beard, his clothes, clasped his leather portfolio, and thrust himself out into its streets, walking quickly. As he lunged towards his target, he recited to himself the things that he should say, impressing himself once more with his commercial insight, his fragile but arguably quite real success.

Was that? No. He hurried past the man and turned into the street of his brother's shop. Through the reflections on the glass, behind the ranked jars of pastilles, the bottles of Oswald's useless tonics that compromised the prestige of Allen's name, he glimpsed his brother's bald head moving. He wiped his palms on his trousers, grasped the door knob, and woke the shop's hysterical little bell with his entrance.

Oswald looked up, looked at him as Matthew

struggled to smile, looked directly into his eyes and saw in his brotherly, intimate, presumptuous way Matthew's purpose. He looked away and as he turned jars on the counter to align their labels precisely outwards said, 'My renowned, respectable brother. But I have no fatted calf for your return . . .'

'Oswald.'

'I told you some time ago.'

'Please, a moment.'

'There is nothing I can do.'

'No, no. It is good news really that I have . . .'

'There is nothing . . .'

Matthew slapped the counter. He shocked himself with the noise and stared down at his bright shoes.

'I have come a long way . . .'

'There is nothing I can do.'

'You'd send me to prison.'

'I'm not sending you anywhere. There is nothing I can do.'

*   *   *

Matthew sat back in his chair, his book of imaginary numbers open before him. His eyes rested, unseeing, on the orrery by the window. He sank into a feeling of humiliation. It had an unclean warmth, like pissed-into bath water. The orrery slowly grew into his sight. When he noticed it, his thoughts swam away into philosophy. Those small globes on the end of the arms suspended in the vastness of space, in a total silence, and life, as far as man knew, on only one of those small globes, a mere dust adhering to its surface, and to what

225

end? He achieved a deeply peaceful dejection, a sad smile on his face, thinking of man's short squirming frenzy before entering the silence. He knew that chaos, that consequences would soon follow, so he took a careful pleasure in this time alone in his study, his neat figures drying on the ledger, the letter refolded, his last hope gone. So when the study door was flung open, Matthew Allen stood up immediately.

'What is this I hear?' Tennyson shouted. 'What is this I hear?'

'I don't know,' Matthew Allen answered. 'I'm afraid you're going to have to tell me.'

'I most certainly will.' Tennyson stood with his chin raised, head tilted, his hands in his hair, glaring down at the doctor. He was barely in control of himself, rage had so broken up his stillness, filled him with unfamiliar quickness and ferocity. He spoke with precision to keep it under control, holding on to his hair. 'I have just spoken to my brother. He informed me, with some reluctance, as one with a horror of unnecessary suffering and disturbance, that some time ago you asked him for money, when all along it had been made perfectly clear to you that Septimus would not invest in your scheme.'

'That is true. I did offer him the opportunity to involve some funds in our scheme in expectation of future . . .'

'Because you were short of money. Because your imbecile machine is not making money. Meanwhile I am receiving letters from other members of my family anxiously enquiring after the dividends that should now be being paid. And from you there comes nothing, and more nothing.'

226

'Please be calm. Allow me to show you my accounts.' Now was the time for them, finally, after all the scrupulous work. Allen picked up the ledger and stepped towards the irate poet. Tennyson grabbed him by the shoulder and pushed him back.

'Enough talkee, talkee, as the niggers say. I don't want to see your numbers. I want the first dividend to be paid. I have trusted you. You are into my family for eight thousand pounds and now you ask Septimus for a thousand more?' Tennyson was very strong. Allen, now hollowed by illness, hung from Tennyson's hand as the big, dirty, wide-mouthed face bore down on him. He almost liked it, the cringe of fear in his genitals. He wanted to lean into the blast of his rage, to be purified by it, to be destroyed. 'My father is dead,' Tennyson was saying. 'What we have invested is our inheritance and we appear to be losing it. For months you have flannelled and promised.'

'Family money. That family that weighs you down. You might be grateful.'

'What business is that of yours?'

'You will get your money back and many times more. It just needs a little time.'

'I thought you were out of the run of common men, not one of the herd. I trusted you. But evidently you are one of the herd, mutton-headed. Greasy and commercial and incapable.'

'I'm not. Please let me go.'

'Mercantile in spirit. Petty. A swindler.' Tennyson shook the man with both hands. Allen clasped the ledger to his chest, his eyelids fluttering in the big man's breath. 'I'll not let you ruin me, Matthew Allen. You will make good your debts to me, to all of us. Why, why have you done this?'

'I haven't. I won't. I am your friend. Here, yes, here's an idea: life insurance, on me, as an absolute guarantee.'

'Of what?'

'Of moneys returning to you.'

'For which I'll need you dead?'

*   *   *

Crusoe began to consider his position and the circumstances he was reduced to on the island. For clarity, he set good against evil like debtor and creditor, scribbling in his notebook, the pages crinkled by dried sea water.

Evil: I am without defence, or means to resist any violence of madman or sane man or beast.

Good: I am a hardy fighter of great reputation and can answer for myself with my fists.

Evil: Since my shipwreck I have been denied the love of my wives, the satisfaction of manly desire, the smiles of my children.

Good: There is good provender. Food requires little foraging.

Evil: I am all alone.

Evil: I am not where I should be, not in my home.

Evil: I am tormented by memories and phantasies and spells of insensibility.

Evil: My verses languish unread and unheard by any man.

Good: Nature is my mother and is here as elsewhere, although she wears a strange face so far from the scenes I love.

Evil: I want my Mary.

Evil: I may die here and I want Mary and I half-wish I had died in the storm on the sea.

*   *   *

Beeswax and lavender. It was the smell of the house that affected Hannah most strongly. The linens, the upholstery were fragrant with herbs and a dim, soothing aroma rose from the polished wood. In the vestibule, a potted hyacinth had cast its strong perfume, like a bright lamp's light, into the air. The house may have been small, but it was wonderfully tight and tidy and quiet. The carpets were new, with a pattern that curled across deep red, and they stood up on the floorboards almost an inch tall. There was sunlight through the bay window where they sat and all the teacups steamed gold.

It was no surprise that Dora should excel as a wife, but the comfort Hannah felt was a surprise. She hadn't thought she would like it so much. James was taking an evident pride in the respectable charms of his marital home, smiling to himself as things were admired. Dora was less at ease, vigilant of her siblings and tense for each part of the ceremony. She widened her eyes meaningfully when Fulton, having finished his piece of cake, sat back wiping his mouth with his napkin and inhaling deeply through his nose. Watching Dora try and chastise Fulton in silence made Hannah feel mischievous. She teased her older sister.

'I hope this is your best set of china. I remember there were two at the wedding.'

'Of course it is.'

Hannah felt a blush chase up her neck into her face. She was instantly ashamed. Dora's snappish reply was perfectly in order. There was nothing here to be mocked. In fact, there was much that was considerable. Dora had always wanted quiet and decency and here it was. Dora had not asked about events at home because she did not want to know. The inventories being made, the sale of goods, were repugnant to her. She didn't even ask about her father's poor health because of what that invoked. She did not feel she had to know. She and James were a new generation, in a new home. There they would be safe from her parents' extravagance and failures and would never meet another patient.

Fulton asked James polite questions about his work in the bank.

'This is such a lovely window,' Hannah said to Dora.

'Yes,' Dora answered. 'It catches all of the afternoon sun.'

To love the life that was possible: that also was a

freedom, perhaps the only freedom. A place like this was possible. Hannah could love such a life, the safety, the calm, her own children. Charles Seymour had sent her a letter after he'd fled. He thanked her for their conversation out picking blackberries. She had reminded him to be courageous. She had set him off with her words. He had misunderstood her completely and gone. She had read the letter once and burned it and cried alone.

She cut a triangle of cake with her fork and ate.

*　　　*　　　*

Abigail had grown. She knew she had because, running up the stairs, she was at eye level with the soaring diagonal of the dado rail. There were shelves in the larder she could now reach, resulting in Cook keeping currants at a safer altitude. She could see over tabletops and there she found her parents' faces, tight, preoccupied, with flat, unseeing eyes.

She ran to her father's side and put her hand on his knee. He looked down at her with those dull rabbit eyes and said, 'Not now, child.' Abigail tilted her head downwards, leaned back, and looked flirtatiously up past her eyebrows at him in the way that usually softened her parents, softened anyone, and brought them smiling towards her. No response. She swayed closer to take hold of his ear and squeeze it together, but he gave his head an angry horse's shake. 'Child, you will not deflect me.'

Abigail's mother entered the room and Abigail's father sank a little in his chair and coughed.

Abigail could see—anyone could see—that he was making his malady look worse to get her mother's sympathy. Indeed, Eliza stood behind him and ran a hand across the great width of coat stretched over his back. He coughed again as she did so. Abigail would have sympathised as well, but he didn't seem to want her. He wanted Mama. Eliza didn't look happy either and Abigail walked around and rested herself affectionately against her skirt. As a reward, her mother dropped a hand onto her shoulder. Abigail always tried to cheer people up, to make them happier, and she always would. She would live devotedly with her mother long after her father's illness, which, although exaggerated at this moment, was real and would soon kill him. Finally she would migrate to a marriage in which her husband was never as kind to her as he might have been, having no need to be.

'I'm not sure we can part with any more,' her mother said to her father.

Her father coughed with tightly closed lips, then said, 'They won't leave us a stick. All these years of work. Not a matchstick. These Tennysons will have it all.'

Fulton entered then and stared with naked disgust at the sad gazes that met his, said nothing and went out, slamming the door.

*   *   *

Swish of leaves, of strong drink. One of them idly compressing a squeezebox, not playing, but pushing out a few quiet notes. The broth with hare's meat hung over the fire, bubbles lumping up to the surface. And opposite, a row of the girls deft

232

with short knives cutting pegs to sell, quick as coring apples.

Judith was telling him of the two missing men.

'Said we's an atrocious tribe and that we ought to be made outlaws from every civilised kingdom. These are his words I'm telling you. And that we ought to be exterminated from the face of the earth. Exterminated.'

'And him a clergyman.'

'A Christian man.'

'Or pretends to be,' said John.

'That's it. Or pretends to be. It was common land a few months back and what grew and bred on it was common as God's air. Now it's the railway's and the boys are gaoled. And you could only tell it from signs they couldn't read, not having the art. Now it's chavvies without their fathers.'

'When will they be out?'

She shook her head as though they never would be, then said, 'A year or two. Less, maybe, I reckon.'

'And you're all going away.'

'Forest is a good place for us, good for food, but we've had too many night visits, been shaken in our vardas, and their dogs going mad. So now it's down to Kent for a fair. We want to, matter of fact. All our people gather.'

'To have fun at the fair.'

'Not me,' Judith answered. 'I'll talk is all I'll do, maybe tell the odd fortune. One time of day, I used to get up at four o'clock in the morning. I could run or jump or do anything you mention. But today I'm useless. That one, she'll have a livelier time of it.' She pointed with her pipe stem at one of the peg-making girls. 'She'll be seeing her lover boy there. See, the passion's gone to her hands. Look at the mess she's making.'

If the girl could hear, she pretended otherwise, whispering behind her hand to the girl on her left.

'He'll be there, will he?' John asked immediately, unreasonably jealous.

'He will. They haven't see each other since they were not but nine years old, the pair of them, but they made promises and their words have been passed along in the meantime, their messages to each other, from mouth to ear between the travelling people, and now his people will be in Kent same as us.'

'I see.' John took another swig. 'Got to go for a moment,' he said, and stood up.

Soft light flaking through the leaves. He unbuttoned himself and let his stream go between the thick, down-diving roots of a hornbeam, his belly resting on his right foream. He thought about the girl, her love, the lovers' separate paths through the world that now would join, reuniting them, fusing at last. The excitement that must be in her breast, the pure passion! In John as well, the loneliness, the wandering and desire for home, for Mary. How she'd stayed true and steadfast while all the world went wrong. He felt his toes wet and looked down to see his puddle rolling against his boots. What a fool's mistake: to piss uphill! This is what came of living between walls and pissing always into china. He dried his toecaps, digging furrows on the ground.

As he thrashed back through the branches, he called, 'Which way out is it? Tell me. Which way out of the forest?'

'Out? Where to?'

'North. To Northampton.'

'North is the Enfield road.'

'How would I find that then?'

'We can leave you signs if you like, before we go. Ties on branches to show you the way.'

'You will do it?'

'If you like.'

'I do. Our secret, though?'

'Our secret? We are secret. We don't talk.'

'And I'll find them?'

'You'll find 'em, no fear.'

*   *   *

'There's every chance, I suppose.'

'You suppose?'

'Well,' Thomas Rawnsley shifted in his chair, 'your husband has entered a marketplace which is new to everybody.'

'So, he can't know,' Fulton said and stared into his mother's worried eyes.

'No, he can't know precisely. None of us can. But that's not to say . . .'

'If it were your company, would you have proceeded in the same manner?'

'Fulton, don't interrogate out guest.'

'But would you?'

'I . . .' Rawnsley raised his hands, glanced across at the silent Hannah. 'Broadly, yes, I suppose I would.'

'So, why are you a success and . . .'

'Fulton!'

'Your father is a very ingenious man, of that I have no doubt.'

The doubts he did have sat in the air. Fulton

235

stared at the carpet, thinking.

'But it wasn't especially to discuss Dr Allen that I came.'

'Oh, no?' Eliza enquired.

'No. I wanted, if I may, to speak to Hannah.'

'I see.'

Hannah felt all their eyes on her and blushed painfully. Why did he have to announce it and make this public show? Now her mother and brother were getting up to leave them alone, as though she were about to be examined by a doctor and required privacy.

'We shall leave you two alone, then,' her mother said.

Hannah glanced up and met her mother's gaze. She had her tongue tip between her teeth in that idiotic expression. Hannah looked down again quickly, clenched her teeth, felt her lips harden into a line.

The door closed behind them. The room was silent. They were alone.

'Well,' Rawnsley began, and stopped. He placed one hand emphatically on the table as though about to begin again, but didn't. He drummed his fingers.

Why did he have to do this now? Why not when he was more alive and engaging? He could be, she knew that. Instead, he looked in Hannah's direction, but not at her, and drummed his fingers. Eventually he said, 'Why don't we go for a walk? It would be nice to be outside, don't you think?'

'Yes, it would.'

So now they too went out and left the room empty. The fact that nobody was now in the room felt like another awkwardness to Hannah, although

236

she couldn't have said why. She thought of its silence and empty stillness as they went into the hall.

Thomas Rawnsley helped her into her coat, waited while she buttoned her gloves.

The breeze was cool, but not strong. There were small leaves on half of the trees and clouds in the sky. An ordinary day. It gave no sign that anything special, any event, was occurring.

Rawnsley, clasping his hands in the small of his back, led away from the house. Then at a certain distance, perhaps with a particular view onto the lane and forest in mind, he stopped.

'You know that I have come to admire you very much, Hannah,' he began.

'Of course,' she snapped back. 'The flowers. The visits.'

He shook his head, as if interrupted, muttering to himself. He started again. 'You know that I have come to admire you very much, Hannah.' Hannah could see that he had it all rehearsed in his mind, this spot, these words, and that his seriousness, his apparent lack of pleasure, was because he wanted it very much to happen in exactly the right way. She had the power, evidently, to conform to his dream, to allow his imaginings to be realised. She, who'd wasted so many of her own fantasies, could grant him that, and suddenly she very much wanted to.

'I would like your permission to ask your father for his permission,' he blinked, as if unsure whether the sentence made sense, 'for his permission to ask for your hand in marriage.'

'Yes.'

'Hannah. Would you consent to becoming my

wife?'

Hannah smiled, answering honestly, 'I would.'

'Ah!' he smiled, raised two fists, then controlled himself. Apparently the business was unfinished, there was more of his dream to accomplish. 'May I . . . may I kiss your hand?'

Hannah widened her eyes as her heart beat heavily at these words. Sighing and kissing at last. 'Yes,' she whispered, 'you may,' and held out her right hand.

Thomas Rawnsley reached for it with both of his own, and without saying anything turned it over and unbuttoned her glove. This too must have been part of the dream. She watched as he gently pulled the glove from her hand, held it still upturned in his own, bent forward, and with a warm crush of breath and beard against her skin, kissed her palm, then closed her fingers over the kiss as though he had given her a coin.

*　　　*　　　*

He smoked as he piled his books. He puffed with small pursings of his lips and read the spines. *Purgatorio*. He hadn't got up enough Italian to read Dante. Of course he hadn't. He never would. He would return to Somersby and would fail to do so there also, sinking into the place to dissolve, as smoke merges upwards into the air. The family shadows would surround him, their black blood would continue to circulate in his veins. There was no escape. He was the equal of any English poet, but he took with him a wallet that contained half-finished things only and had new ones about Arthur in his throat, but none of that made a

238

difference. Eventually, if they were published, the critics would decry them again and there would be no Hallam to rise to his defence. No, he returned with nothing. He'd tried the world, tried enterprise, and now was bankrupt, his money gone into the mad doctor's mad scheme. It was a humiliation. Worse, he had to return to the family home and live narrowly. He'd believed the doctor's delusions, he'd written some poems and that was that. He remained the same stale person. He would finish packing up his books. The servants would straighten the place after him, pluck out the creases he had made. He would go back to Somersby to smoke and dwindle and, when his spirits allowed, to begin the poem about Arthur.

*   *   *

Hannah did not listen to what her father was saying. Seated beside her at the organ, her mother did. Head dropped forward, Eliza stared at the red, curled fingers in her lap. Hannah had discovered her sitting alone like this a few times recently. The posture tightened her mother's narrow shoulders, made her look girlish and chastised. And then quickly she would be up and active again.

Hannah stared vaguely at the stops of the organ, bone-white, labelled with their voices, a litany that ran jingling through her mind whenever she sat there to turn the pages: Clarion. Bombard. Contra Posaune. Mixture. Gemshorn. Dulciana. Trumpet. It did so now, although not in the usual infuriating way it usually did, but happily, like birdsong in the background as she thought about the letter from

Thomas Rawnsley in her dressing table, his promises, her future.

'Affliction separates man from man,' Dr Allen said. His hands gripped the sides of the lectern. He looked down at the mad and told them, 'That is part of its purpose. It is sent us from God to force us to resort to Him, to see that He is our one true refuge, to lead us from the unreliable inconstancy of our fellow men to the sanctuary of Christ.'

Margaret stared at the speaking man. The red in his eyes was a giveaway: they had made their habitation within him as well. But he needn't fear. She ought to tell him that. Even if they destroyed his mortal body, he need not fear. All would be well. It had been vouchsafed. It was near at hand. Her own release was only the beginning. The joy of it burned inside her.

Hannah was startled out of her thoughts when her mother's hands flew up and started shaping themselves over the keys. Behind them the variable voices jostled together.

William Stockdale oversaw the patients' departure.

George Laidlaw once again fervently shook the doctor's hand. 'Thank you,' he said. 'Thank you. I cannot tell you what comfort you give.'

'I am glad of it,' Allen said, gathering his papers, and George Laidlaw reluctantly hobbled away to his endless guilty calculations of the National Debt.

*   *   *

Away, towards home, at last, at last, he walked. He touched his hat to Peter Wilkins who, opening

240

the gate for him, tilted his intricate face in acknowledgement. He walked out onto the path, into the forest. When he got to the place they were gone, as they said they might be. The vardas were gone, the horses. They had kicked loose stuff of the forest floor over the soft scorched heap of the fire. A wide-brimmed hat lay on the ground. It shuddered in a breeze not quite strong enough to lift it. It provoked a melancholy emotion, looking at that hat, but he had no time for it. There were no signs, no ribbons tied to anything he could see. Friendly and lawless and unreliable, they'd upped and gone. He crouched for a moment, read north from the shadows and the green side of the trees, and set off. Flickering shadows, the endlessly breaking fence of trees. He just had to keep walking, boring through, shouldering the distance with the low grunting strength of a badger, and he would get there, he would be home and free, with Mary. He was right, at least partly: Mary was dead, but he would get back and find his wife, his home, his life, and would stay there for a short time until his mind broke and he was again unmanageable. He would be taken then to Northampton Lunatic Asylum, which he would never leave. The remaining twenty-three years of his life would be spent inside those walls. He would die there, no longer a poet, obscure and incarcerated.

He left the forest, the doctor, the other patients, Stockdale's tortures behind him. He broke through the incessant rushing sound of the trees into silence. A day. A breeze blew softly against him. He had to choose a road for Enfield and took the wrong one. He asked at a public house and was set on the right way. After Enfield it was the Great

York Road, walking north until dark.

At dusk, he was staggering. He should have taken food, water at least, but that would have looked suspect. His knees were weak with sharp pains at their centres. He saw a paddock with a pond and a yard beyond it. He scaled the rotting fence, walked a wide margin around the pond for fear of falling in and drowning, and crept into the yard. Inside he found a fine bed of baled clover, six feet by six. He lay on it, the motion of the walk fading out of his exhausted limbs. He kept drifting down onto the bed like a bird landing from a height, kept sinking down onto it. He slept uneasily and dreamed that Mary lay by his side, but was taken from him. He awoke still in darkness and alone. He thought he'd heard someone say 'Mary,' but when he searched the place there was nobody there. He looked up at the stars to find the pole star. He lay down again with his head pointing towards it so he would know the direction to walk immediately that he woke again.

He awoke in daylight and late, with the mist burned away and the dew drying, but nevertheless he hadn't been seen. He thanked God and got back onto the road.

Walking, head down, ignoring the occasional carts, counting milestones he passed. Soon he would have to drink something, to eat, would have to find a way to eat.

He removed his boots to shake out the gravel that was cutting him, the soles now worn down to paper and starting to tear. Passing the other way, towards London, a man on horseback said, 'Here's another of the broken-down haymakers,' and threw down a penny. It sparkled on the path. John picked it up and called thanks after him. He exchanged the coin for half a pint in a pub called The Plough, finding refuge there from a heavy shower that pelted the thick, uneven glass of the pub's windows.

Setting off again, he seemed to pass milestones very quickly, but by nightfall they had been stretched by hunger and exhaustion further and further apart. He stopped in a village and decided to call at a house to get a light for his pipe, having no matches, and there find the parson to fall upon his charity. An old woman allowed him into the parlour where a young girl sat making lace over a cushion and a gentleman smoked and stared. He asked them the way to the parson's house, but they wouldn't answer. Was his voice making a sound at all? He certainly heard it. The old woman brought him a lit taper. He sucked the flame in, growing light-headed. The girl said something with her head lowered. The man smiled.

On the road again, he found a countryman, chatty and amenable, on his way to catch a coach, who told him the parson lived a long way off, too far to walk. John asked if there was shelter nearby, a barn maybe, with dry straw. The man told him The Ram Inn would do and said to follow him. John didn't make it far, however, before he had to rest on a pile of flint. His stomach was burningly empty, his legs refusing. The man was kind and lingered, but when he heard the church bells hastened after his coach.

John walked on, but couldn't find the inn. He lay down to rest in the shade of a row of elms, but the wind blew through them and prevented sleep. He got up in the dusk to find somewhere better. The odd houses spaced along the road were lit up within, snug and separate.

Finally he came to The Ram but, having no money, did not go in. There was a shed that leaned against one end of it, but with people passing he didn't dare try and sneak in. Instead, he walked. The road was dark and darker still where trees overshadowed, thrashing softly in the wind.

He came to a crossing of two turnpikes and in his exhaustion could not calculate which way was north and which south. He chose by not choosing, by starting to walk, and soon became sure he had made an error and was heading back the way he had come, heading back to it all, to Fairmead House, to Leopard's Hill Lodge and the dark forest. He heard himself whimpering with the misery, almost too feeble to keep walking, shuffling forward in the dark. He almost felt he was not moving at all, lifting his feet up and down in infinite darkness. Eventually a light hung in the air, dipping and rising with his steps. A tollgate. His eyes cringed at its fierce brightness when he got to the door and knocked. A man emerged with a candle, peering and unfriendly, the candle's flame streaming sideways. John asked if he was heading north. 'After that gate you are,' the man said and shut his door.

New strength flowed into John. As he walked he hummed an old song, 'Highland Mary'. Singing her name. Getting closer.

His strength guttering out again. When he found a house by the road with a large porch, he crept in and lay down. He found it long enough to lie with his knotted legs straight out. He reminded himself to wake before the inhabitants did. He rested

244

himself against the warmth of the place, like a child against its mother. All the inhabitants were asleep. He could hear their snores, the creak of straw mattresses.

He woke up at dawn feeling strong. The west was white and blue. Overhead, into the east, a cobbled road of bright rose clouds. He blessed his two wives, his daughter Queen Victoria, and set off again.

After some miles, he rested by an estate wall. From its lodge gate emerged a tall gypsy woman. He asked her where he was and she told him. She had an honest, handsome face. They walked together to the next town and she sang under her breath. She told him to put something inside his hat to hold the crown up. 'You'll be noticed,' she said. When she left him to take her separate way she told him of a shortcut via a church, but he didn't dare take it for fear, in his starvation and fatigue, of getting confused and losing his way.

Around him the world weakened, started vanishing. There was only the beat of pain from his feet, his hunger, his hands heavy and throbbing by his side. A dyke ran along a roadside field. He stumbled in to get some sleep. He woke and found himself wet down one side. He got up and carried on into darkness, into night, into dimensionless dark.

In the morning he had an idea. He got onto his hands and knees and began eating the damp grass. Sweet and plain, it was not unlike bread. There was something else he could eat, he realised, and pulled the tobacco from his pocket and chewed as he walked, drinking down the bitter saliva, eventually swallowing the whole thing down.

He kept going. It was hard to walk in a straight line. Around him the town of Stilton arose. Halfway through it, he rested on a gravel causeway and heard a young woman's voice say, 'Poor creature.' An older woman's voice answered, 'Oh, he shams.' He got up then and as he staggered to his feet the old woman said, 'Oh, no he don't.' He didn't look back to see them. He walked on.

At the other end of town he gathered his strength to ask a young woman, 'Is this the right road for Peterborough?' 'Yes,' she said. 'This is the Peterborough road.' Home. He was almost home. He rubbed the tears from his nose.

Just outside Peterborough, a man and a woman in a cart called to him. They were old neighbours from his infancy's village of Helpston. They'd recognised him. He bent over and held his knees and called to them that he hadn't eaten or drunk since he'd left London. They found fivepence between them and threw it down. He picked it up from the road, thanking them, waving his ruined hat as they drove away.

A small pub by a bridge over a noisy stream. Inside, the fivepence became twopence of bread and cheese and two half-pints. He dozed as he chewed, struggling to keep his eyes open, but in a little while the food had dispersed into him as strength. Starting to walk again, the pain from his torn feet was sharpened by the rest, but he was too near home now to sit down on the road—he would have been ashamed to do it lest he be seen by people he knew.

Peterborough. Streets. Windows. People. Horses. Peterborough dwindling behind him. Then Walton. Then Werrington. A few miles only to go. A cart

246

stopped beside him. It carried a man, a woman and a boy. 'Get in,' they told him, but he refused; he was so close, they needn't bother for him. But the woman kept insisting with a passion that made him suspect she was drunk or mad. 'It's Patty,' she said. 'It's Patty, your wife. Get in.' They hauled him up onto the cart and he lay on his back to be carried the final miles home. He stared up at the clouds that moved with them. He felt the rough pressure of Patty's kisses on his face. 'John,' Patty said. 'Poor John. You're almost home. You're here.' He'd made it. It was all behind him. Patty wiped the dirt from his face with her heavy clean hand. She stroked his head. His legs twitched. He turned his face into the smell of her. He licked his cracked lips. 'Patty,' he whispered. 'Patty.'

'That's right. Almost home.'

'Mary.'

ACKNOWLEDGEMENTS

Of the many books and journals consulted for this novel, I would like to acknowledge particularly Jonathan Bate's *John Clare*, Roger Sales' *John Clare: A Literary Life*, Robert Bernard Martin's *Tennyson: The Unquiet Heart*, and Pamela Faithfull's PhD thesis *Matthew Allen MD, chemical philosopher, phrenologist, pedagogue and mad-doctor, 1783–1845*. Readers of these historical works will know that in shaping this material as fiction I have taken a number of liberties, compressing events that occurred over several years into the space of seven seasons and ignoring some significant individuals while inventing others.

CHIVERS LARGE PRINT –direct–

If you have enjoyed this Large Print book and would like to build up your own collection of Large Print books, please contact

Chivers Large Print Direct

Chivers Large Print Direct offers you a full service:

● Prompt mail order service

● Easy-to-read type

● The very best authors

● Special low prices

For further details either call Customer Services on (01225) 336552 or write to us at Chivers Large Print Direct, **FREEPOST**, Bath BA1 3ZZ

Telephone Orders: **FREEPHONE** 08081 72 74 75